# The Tales of Fluke & Tash

# Christmas Adventure

To ELIZA

HAPPY CHRISTMAS !

M.

Fluke and Tash series:

Robin Hood Adventure

Egyptian Adventure

Ancient Greece Adventure

Dinosaur Adventure

Christmas Adventure

# The Tales of Fluke & Tash

# Christmas Adventure

## MARK ELVY

Available from

www.ypdbooks.com
and
www.flukeandtash.com

© Mark Elvy, 2019

Published by Fluke & Tash Publishing

A CIP catalogue record for this book is available from the British Library.

ISBN 978-1-9998910-3-9

Book layout by Clare Brayshaw

Prepared and printed by:

York Publishing Services Ltd
64 Hallfield Road
Layerthorpe
York YO31 7ZQ

Tel: 01904 431213

Website: www.yps-publishing.co.uk

17th December

# The North Pole...

The letter, sealed inside a small, white envelope and stuck down with sticky tape, had nearly reached its final destination. The handwriting on the front, big and bold in thick red crayon, had six words, scribbled hastily in hope and anticipation:

## Santa Claus's Workshop
## The North Pole

The top right-hand corner of the envelope, where a stamp would normally be glued, was left blank. In its place was a small sketch in crayon of a bunch of green holly and red berries. The sender had either forgotten the stamp, couldn't afford one or didn't think it necessary.

Thankfully, letters to this address didn't need a stamp, postal service, courier or any type of postman, the sender just needed belief in the spirit of Christmas and kindness.

This residence received letters from all around the world. Large typed ones from a computer, small but carefully crafted letters where the words had been chosen with thought through to hastily written letters on scruffy bits of paper without any envelope.

It didn't matter. All the letters were treated with the same respect.

Elfred, the Chief Postal Elf, looked around the post room. It was the same every year. Hectic. Especially with only one week to go to the big day, but he wouldn't have it any other way. It was his responsibility to ensure each letter received was processed and passed to Santa Claus, Father Christmas, St Nicholas, Krissy Kringle and a whole bunch of other names for the big man, his boss, or just Santa as he called him.

Elfred looked out the small window of his post room. He never tired of the view. To his left was Santa's toy workshop, a large sprawling log-built cabin, the building a buzz of activity all year round, but this time of the year it was in operation twenty four hours a day, seven days a week. Further back he could see the reindeer school and stables.

To his right were fantastic views across the courtyard to the Elf school. Young Elves slowly trudging through the snow, throwing the occasional snowball, satchels slung over their shoulders, heading into class for the day.

He looked to see if he could see his son. Little Elfonzo would be there somewhere, probably getting into mischief before school started for the day. Well, he is an Elf, and Elves are full of harmless fun and mischief; that's what Elves do when they're young, play pranks and silly games on each other – and anybody else that gets too close!

Elf school teaches you manners and sets you up for a long career working with Santa. The options are endless at the workshop. He remembered his days at Elf school, fascinated by the lectures and classes the teachers gave, explaining in great detail the importance of becoming a fully trained Elf.

Elfred heard a faint rumbling noise. The hatch in one of the walls opened, revealing two long chutes leading up to the sky. He glanced out the window and strained his neck to look skywards. 'Yep, here they come, today's delivery of post,' he said to himself as he watched a huge bundle of loose letters come tumbling down the magic chutes and into the post room, scattering themselves into the base of two large wooden trollies. One chute led to a trolley marked "Naughty" which had a few letters in the bottom, the second chute led directly to a trolley marked "Nice" and which was near to overflowing.

The main door to the post room creaked as it was opened from outside. A large, bearded man entered, stamping his feet to remove any excess snow from his boots. He was in good humour this morning, dishing out *hellos* and *good mornings* to all the post room Elves, as the portly figure made his way over to the large wooden trollies.

The first thing Elfred noticed about the newcomer, in fact the first thing everybody noticed, was an amazing, bushy, white beard.

'Good morning Elfred, I see the daily post has arrived!' said the voice through the bushy, white beard.

'How do you manage to do it?' laughed Elfred, looking up as his boss, Santa Claus, walked over to the large pile of envelopes stacked to overflowing in the "Nice" trolley and peered inside.

'Manage to do what?' chuckled Santa, looking down at the mountain of letters.

'Every morning, without fail, you time your entry just as the post arrives. It's as if you have magic powers. The letters whisper to you that they're here, ready and waiting for you to inspect them,' chuckled Elfred, knowing full well that Santa was indeed actually magic. Anybody that could run this place, or *Santa's workshop*, as it was more commonly known, must have special powers.

Santa tapped the side of his nose with his gloved finger. 'Plenty of practice, Elfred. As you know, we've been running this operation for a long time, a very long time indeed, so I should know by now what time the post arrives,' chuckled Santa.

Just before Santa closed the wooden shutter he glanced up at one of the chutes, frowned, and asked Elfred to pass him a long stick.

'What's the matter?' asked Elfred.

'Something's got stuck, wedged in the chute just at the point where the magic sorts out whether the letter should be sent to the "Naughty" or "Nice" trolley.' Santa wiggled and poked the letter with his stick, and watched as it fluttered down the chute, before hovering for a few seconds above both trollies. Undecided which trolley to land in, it gave up and fluttered onto the workbench directly in front of Santa.

'In all our years of working here, we rarely, if ever, see that happening!' said Elfred.

Santa removed his glove, reached down and picked up the letter, studied the front and chuckled when he saw the red crayon, scribbled neatly on the front:

# Santa Claus's Workshop
# The North Pole

'Intriguing...' whispered Santa, nodding 'a very rare occurrence. I agree, in all our years....' His voice trailed off as he opened his jacket and placed the letter carefully inside his top pocket. 'I'll take this one back to my study and read it with my morning tea and biscuits. Mrs Claus is making me a brew in a few minutes – tea and homemade cookies. I can't be late and upset the good Mrs Claus. I'll have a cup ready and waiting for you when you deliver both trollies of letters to me later this morning,' and he turned and walked through another door, heading out into the cold.

Elfred watched through the window as Santa strolled across the courtyard to continue his daily rounds, making his way over to the toy workshop.

# Santa writes a letter...

Santa sat in his comfy armchair, having first removed his boots, which were left by the back door to dry. Mrs Claus brought in a pot of tea, two mugs, and a plate stacked high with homemade biscuits. She settled down by the log fire, wiggling and warming her toes, sighed contentedly, sipped her tea and watched her husband.

'Thank you dearest,' mumbled Santa, reaching for a biscuit and dunking it into his hot tea. He opened the intriguing envelope and unfolded the letter inside. He reached for his spectacles, perched them on the end of his nose, and read the letter out loud to Mrs Claus.

'*Dear Mr and Mrs Claus...*' he started to read the letter and looked up.

'It's not very often I get a mention,' said Mrs Claus, happily munching on her biscuit.

'*We would love to come to your workshop at the North Pole and help this Christmas,*' Santa continued. '*We know it's a very busy time of the year for you and the Elves. We don't need paying, but my friend has asked for a large bag of dog biscuits if possible....*'

'Dog biscuits?' frowned Mrs Claus, 'who feeds their children dog biscuits?'

Santa carried on reading. *'Please, please let us help. It will be a great adventure! We've both been good this year, although sometimes my friend can be a little bit naughty. We hope to receive a reply. Kind regards, Fluke and Tash.'*

'That'll be why the letter hovered between the "Naughty" and "Nice" trollies,' chuckled Santa, 'ones been good, the other has been a little bit naughty.' He tore a page from his official Santa's workshop notepad, thought carefully and began to write. *'Dear Fluke and Tash....'* He wrote several lines in his neat handwriting. Satisfied with his reply, he popped the letter into an envelope, licked it and sealed it shut, ready to be posted.

'They'll never find us out here in our magic workshop. So many people have tried but we're invisible to everybody, well most people anyway,' said Mrs Claus, sipping her tea.

'That's true,' confirmed Santa, 'but all you have to do is believe in the Christmas spirit and make a wish, and then you can see right through the invisibility shield that surrounds us. It's a shame, because we could do with the extra help this time of the year.'

Mrs Claus nodded and agreed, 'yes, especially in the kitchen. We've got hundreds of hungry

Elves to feed every day. Nigelfa, our head cook, is snowed under!'

Santa finished his tea and got up out of the armchair, stretched, and headed for the door. Pausing at the magic chimney, he released the letter and watched as it disappeared. 'No rest, dear,' he smiled, turning to his wife. 'I better go and check on the reindeer. Randolph wasn't feeling too good yesterday. We can't have him feeling ill, not this time of the year.'

## 18th December – England

# Snowball fight...

Fluke was sat at the patio door gazing in excitement through the glass. This was his first winter. Yesterday when he went to bed the grass was green, and this morning the whole garden was a dazzling, brilliant white. Everywhere he looked it was the same. White patio; white tree branches; white grass; white garden furniture and a white fence. As he continued to gaze around, he noticed a white figure, standing still, at the top of the garden.

'Tash!' hollered Fluke, not taking his eyes off the stationary figure. No reply. 'Tash, where are you?' Silence. 'She must be still snoozing somewhere,' he said to himself as he fumbled with the key to open the patio door, desperate to see who the newcomer stood in their garden was.

A blast of cold, fresh air greeted him. Fluke shivered and stepped outside, straight into a snow drift that covered the patio floor. His paws instantly started to get numb from the cold, so he carefully began to wade through the snow, heading for the garden. Exactly where the patio ended and the grass began was anybody's guess, as the white carpet of fresh snow started at the house and continued right to the top of the garden. He didn't notice the trail of small paw prints in the snow.

He gingerly made his way up the garden. Passing the Nummers tree stump he wondered if they were snug and warm in their little home, but decided he'd knock on their door on his way back down. The newcomer had to be investigated first.

Fluke noticed the figure hadn't moved. The closer he crept the more he could make out the facial features. It had an orange coloured nose, dark eyes and two skinny stick-like arms. The weirdest thing, Fluke noticed, were the legs. Whoever it was, they didn't seem to have any!

'Hello,' said Fluke cautiously, creeping closer and closer. No reply. 'Can I help you? You'll get cold just standing there.' Still no reply.

Fluke heard a rustling in the bushes and turned his head to see who made the noise. He noticed too late, the small, white ball, fly through the air and splat him right in the face. Howls of laughter followed, and out stepped Tash, armed with two more white balls.

'Snowball fight!' she hollered gleefully and promptly pelted Fluke with the snowballs she'd made.

Fluke stood there covered from head to paw in snow; the soft snowballs broke up on impact, the loose snow dribbled down his face and body, until a small mound of snow collected at his paws.

'Thanks!' laughed Fluke, wiping the remaining snow from his face.

'You're meant to move you know Fluke, not just stand still. At least give me a moving target to aim for, not just stand there getting covered in snow,' chuckled Tash.

'Talking of just standing still, who's your new friend?' Fluke nodded to the silent figure.

'Of course, you'll not have met Snowy the Snowman before. I keep forgetting this is your first winter,' said Tash, walking off towards their new guest.

'Snowman?' said Fluke, following Tash. 'Oh, so that's why he has an orange coloured nose, it's a carrot!' laughed Fluke, 'and the eyes are lumps of coal from the fireplace, and I thought the arms were skinny, they're just twigs that have fallen from the tree,' he chuckled.

'I built him this morning whilst you were fast asleep,' confirmed Tash.

'Can I make one?' begged Fluke. 'He has to have a best friend, Tash, and maybe we can make a Snowdog and Snowcat.' The pair busily began to create their new masterpieces.

# Christmas tree...

Fluke and Tash were excited and waited patiently for the delivery. They were going to help decorate the tree with all the glittery lights and shiny decorations that currently filled the boxes covering the living room floor. Dad had been in and out of the garage, struggling with armfuls of boxes that only came out once a year. He'd already been up the ladder outside and an impressive line of twinkling icicle lights now hung across the front and back of the house.

Fluke couldn't resist a peak in one of the boxes. He rummaged around and got tangled up in a line of fairy lights. Tash opened another box and started to play with some shiny baubles, rolling them around the floor, and managed to lose a couple under the sofa.

'It's here!' said Fluke, trying to untangle himself from the string of lights, whilst looking out the window at the lorry that was reversing down the street.

'Who's here?' said Tash, retrieving a shiny bauble from under the sofa.

'The Christmas tree man,' said Fluke excitedly.

'Wow, look at all those trees,' said Tash, and watched as the driver climbed down from his cab and unloaded a huge, bright green, Nordmann Fir Christmas tree, which stood over six feet tall, was very bushy and gave off wonderful aromas.

It smelt Christmassy, and would look Christmassy once the tree had all its lights and baubles on. Fluke arranged the tree lights. Mum tutted to herself and re-arranged them into a different position, but, when her back was turned, Fluke chuckled to himself and moved them back to where he'd first put them.

The tree was placed in the bay window. It took most of the day to finish, but the house looked great, inside and out.

As night fell, Fluke stood in the bay window and looked down the snowy street. Every house was adorned with festive lights, front gardens had nodding reindeer that lit up, every window proudly displayed their Christmas tree lights, and most had hanging icicle lights dangling from their roofs and gutters. It was a special time of year and Fluke was loving every second of it.

The television was turned off, dad went round the house turning off all the tree lights and went to bed leaving the living room in total darkness.

Tash looked at Fluke who was sat by the fireside looking up the chimney.

'What are you doing, Fluke?' she asked.

'Waiting for a letter, Tash. You know the letter we posted up the chimney? Well, surely Santa would have read it by now. I was hoping he might reply, that was all,' said Fluke hopefully.

Fluke waited for ages, staring up the chimney. He returned the next evening and waited a bit longer, then waited even more. In total he waited for nearly a week, but nothing, no letter ever arrived.

## 24th December

# Christmas Eve...

It was Christmas Eve, the preparations were all but done. The fridge was overflowing and stacked to the brim with enough food to feed the whole street and the Christmas goose with all the trimmings was just waiting to be put in the oven tomorrow morning, Christmas morning.

Mum and dad had drifted off to bed, full of sherry and bloated after eating too many sausage rolls, mince pies and chocolates.

Fluke was still sat staring up the chimney hoping for something to drop. He sighed and said sadly, 'Well Tash, maybe I've not been the best behaved dog this year, and that's why we've not received a reply.'

'You've not been bad, Fluke. Mischievous maybe. Getting into trouble occasionally, but not bad,' said Tash trying to comfort Fluke. 'You do know that Santa receives millions and millions of letters each year, Fluke. There was never any guarantee that he would write back....' and then stopped midsentence. A white envelope fluttered down and landed on the hearth.

They both sat side by side, stunned, staring at the letter.

'You open it, Tash,' said Fluke breathlessly.

'No Fluke, it's your first Christmas, you can open it. C'mon, hurry up and read what it says,' insisted Tash, watching in fascination as Fluke reached out a paw and looked at the writing on the front.

'*Fluke and Tash.* No address, just our names,' Fluke whispered. 'How did it find us without an address?' he asked, turning to Tash.

'Christmas magic, Fluke. You just have to believe in the spirit of Christmas, that's what's so wonderful about this time of year,' she said and watched as Fluke eagerly tore open the envelope and started to read the contents.

*'Dear Fluke and Tash. Thank you for writing to us and your kind offer to visit us at the North Pole. We would love for you to visit and help out at this busy and special time of the year. We can't supply you with an address as its top secret, but if you can find your way to the North Pole and truly believe in the Christmas spirit you'll be able to locate our Christmas workshop and village. Just remember, you have to truly believe in the*

*magic of Christmas to be able find us. We'll
be waiting for you both to arrive and will
certainly have plenty of work for you to do.
Kind regards, Mr and Mrs Claus.'*

'Look Fluke, the letter is dated 17th December,
which was last week! It must have got stuck up
the chimney and only just fallen down,' said Tash.

'We can still go though, can't we, Tash?' said
an excited Fluke. 'I know it's Christmas Eve and
Santa probably thinks we're not bothered about
helping...'

'Have you forgotten something, Fluke?'
interrupted Tash with a grin.

'No. Well, I don't think so,' he replied, scratching
his head deep in thought, 'forgotten what,
exactly?'

'Err the magic suitcase?' Said Tash.

'Magic...?' Fluke gasped as he realised what
Tash meant. 'Of course! Our magic suitcase!
We'll set the co-ordinates and time for the 17th
December and go back a week to help. How could
I have forgotten,' he said.

Tash looked at the cuckoo clock to check on
the time. It had just struck midnight and was
now officially Christmas Day. Just. The clock
chimed, the little wooden bird cooped up inside
was released, flew out of the wooden doors to tell
the world that Christmas Day was here.

'C'mon then, Fluke, let's get going. We'll get the case ready and change into whatever costumes the case picks for us,' she said and watched as Fluke tore up the stairs and into the spare room to get their magic case ready.

## 18<sup>th</sup> December

# The North Pole Express...

Tash set the co-ordinates for the North Pole. She didn't know the exact location of Santa's Christmas village so took a guess. They could always get there and fly around a bit until they found the secret location, hopefully. If they didn't find Santa's workshop this would be a very quick adventure. The case lid sprung open and they eagerly delved inside to retrieve their costumes.

'Elves, Tash! The case has picked us an Elf costume to wear,' chuckled Fluke, who stood next to Tash, gazing into the wardrobe door mirror. 'Wow, I can't believe we're going to help Santa at his workshop. So, my little Elf friend, are we ready to go?'

Tash giggled, 'C'mon spotty Elf, put your stripy Elves hat on straight and hop aboard. Next stop Santa's workshop!'

Fluke glanced over to the red illuminated digital clock on the bedside table and said happily, 'the 12:22 North Pole Express is ready to depart,' and whooped with glee as Tash turned the handle three times, the case spun around and they disappeared from the spare room.

The magic suitcase materialised at the North Pole, a vast, snowy wilderness. This time of year was the winter solstice, the sun disappearing completely below the horizon. Pure, white snow that covered the ground tried to brighten things up but between late December and early March the sky was almost completely in darkness.

'Keep a lookout for Santa's workshop, Fluke,' said Tash through half closed eyes. 'We should have used our goggles again,' she muttered, wiping a paw across her eyes and shivering. The cold winter air and the speed they were travelling were making their eyes water.

'What's it look like?' asked Fluke, rubbing his eyes and shaking his head, trying to clear his sight.

'Not sure, Fluke,' confirmed Tash, 'but let's face it, we haven't seen any type of building, so if you spot something, shout to let me know, as there's a fair chance it'll be Santa's workshop.'

They continued to fly around, looking left and right. The first to see Santa's workshop was the prize, both wanting to be the first to spot their destination.

'I'm freezing and can't see a thing,' said Fluke through chattering teeth.

Tash landed their case, turned to Fluke and agreed, 'Yep, it's a bit nippy, isn't it,' and climbed down off the case, 'we'll get an extra coat from out of the case and try and find our goggles to wear, that should help with this cold, biting wind that's making our eyes water.' She waited for Fluke to climb off the other side of the case.

# Snow drift...

Fluke stepped down into the snow and promptly disappeared from sight. Looking up, Tash couldn't see him anywhere, he'd completely vanished.

'Fluke? Fluke, where are you? C'mon, now's not the time to be playing hide and seek,' she said. When she got no reply, she hopped back on the case, peeked over the edge and saw that Fluke had stepped down from the case and into a deep snowdrift. 'What are you doing down there?' said Tash, trying to keep a straight face and not laugh.

'Ha-ha, very funny. So how come your side of the case is OK and mine is in a deep snowdrift?' he complained.

'You need to be more careful,' she giggled, 'I must have landed on a slight mound, the snowdrift is caused by wind blowing the snow up the sides of the hill.' She reached down to give a helping hand.

'Hurry up, Tash, it's really, really fr... fr... freezing down here,' he said, shivering, 'I'll catch a cold if I'm down here much longer.'

Fluke found Tash's outstretched paw and was dragged back up out of the snowdrift and onto the case. Stepping off the other side, he watched as Tash rummaged around inside. Locating the goggles and two jackets with furry linings around the hood, they both gratefully slipped inside their new items of clothing and instantly felt much warmer.

Tash slipped the goggles over her head to keep the wind out of her eyes and then shouted out in alarm. 'Whoa, I can't see a thing. They're frozen up on the inside,' she said stumbling about, paws fumbling with the tight strap trying to get them off again.

'Better not wear these then,' said Fluke, looking at his pair, 'well not unless you've got a can of de-icer in the case, you know the same as dad uses on his car windscreen,' he joked.

Whilst Tash was stumbling around trying to release the straps of the goggles, Fluke took his revenge for a few days earlier. He formed a couple of perfectly round snowballs, and just as Tash freed herself from the tight-fitting goggles, she turned around to say something and a large, cold snowball splatted her right in the face.

'Snowball fight!' hollered Fluke and pelted Tash with the second missile. Tash laughed, made her own, and a game of *who could build the biggest and best snowball* continued for a few minutes until, breathless and gasping, they both called it a draw.

'I love snow,' said Tash merrily, 'but I guess we'd better start to try and find Santa's workshop and get in the warm.' She walked to the front of the case, staring all around, trying to work out which direction to take.

Fluke wanted to throw just one more before they left. He took careful aim and released his last and biggest snowball. It missed Tash by inches, sailed over her shoulder and promptly disappeared from sight. Frowning, he made another and threw it in the same direction. This disappeared as well.

'Where did they go?' Tash asked, and made one herself. Throwing it in the same direction, it also vanished into thin air.

'What's going on?' asked Fluke, stepping around the case to stand beside Tash.

It was then they heard juvenile laughing and sniggering. It sounded like a child's laugh. Tash was about to reply when a hail of perfectly round snowballs appeared out of thin air, covering Fluke and Tash from head to paw. Dumbstruck, they were both lost for words.

'Where... what... who threw them?' Tash finally spoke, wiping the residue snow from her new jacket, bits of snow stuck in the furry lining of her hood.

Fluke shrugged his shoulders and shook his head in disbelief. He slowly walked forward, hoping to see if anybody was stood there.

'Elfonzo, Candysocks, enough!' said an invisible voice from just a few feet in front of them, 'stop scaring our visitors.'

Startled, Fluke stepped backwards and tripped over Tash who was following close behind, and they both fell into a heap on the floor.

# The invisible shield...

'I want to make sure that we both heard voices Fluke, and it wasn't just me,' said Tash, sat on the cold snow staring straight ahead.

'Don't forget the disappearing snowballs Tash, *and* the snowballs that came flying at us from out of nowhere,' said Fluke.

'OK, so it's agreed. Either we're both seeing and hearing things or some invisible person is stood right in front of us,' confirmed Tash.

Fluke nodded and stood up. He reached down, helped Tash stand and they both slowly walked over to where the voices had been heard seconds before hand.

'Err, hi there,' said Fluke quietly. A fit of juvenile giggling could be heard, but nobody replied. Turning to Tash, she only shrugged her shoulders, so he tried again. 'My name's Fluke and this is my friend Tash.'

'They really can't see us, can they?' the invisible person's voice directly in front of them giggled.

Tash put her paws out in front of her and started walking slowly, step-by-step, until her paws vanished. She stopped and looked over to Fluke, who gasped in shock.

'Tash, you've started to disappear, your paws have gone missing. You're turning into the invisible cat!' he walked over and reached out until his paws disappeared from sight as well. Fluke felt somebody or something touch him and shake his outstretched paws, causing him to jump back in surprise.

He watched as Tash padded forward and completely disappeared from sight. Then he heard her gasp and say, 'Wow! Fluke, you've got to see this. Come on through, it's amazing.'

Fluke hesitated briefly, then decided he didn't have a choice but to follow Tash. Picking up their magic case, he took a deep breath, walked forward, and stepped into a wondrous new world.

It was a scene of joy and happiness. A large village with paths and streets were spread out before their very eyes. The village was illuminated by street lamps, burning brightly and casting plenty of light in every direction. Christmas trees lined the footpaths and were wonderfully decorated with twinkling festive lights. Sledges were being used as transport and pulled by reindeer, and hundreds of Elves were scampering around, playing games and shouting to each other gleefully at the top of their voices.

Dwellings of all shapes and sizes were dotted here, there and everywhere. Some of the buildings looked like houses and others looked like workshops. Stood directly in front of them was a small group of Elves, staring up at Fluke and Tash.

Tash turned to Fluke, and with a huge smile she laughed, 'I guess we've found the North Pole and Santa's Christmas village.'

# Santa's Christmas village...

'Welcome to the North Pole,' said one of the Elves. Upon closer inspection the Elf that spoke appeared older than the others. He strode forward, offering his hand in a friendly greeting. Tash shook it and introduced themselves.

'Yes…' smiled the friendly Elf, '…we know who you are. My name's Elfred, and this…' he ruffled one of the younger Elves hair, 'is my son Elfonzo and his friend, Candysocks. Sorry if we startled you, but we were told to expect you, so we've been waiting for you to arrive.'

'How did you know we were coming, and how did you know where and when we would arrive?' asked a bewildered Tash.

'It's Santa's job to know everything about everybody, he's magic you know. He told us you'd be here soon and asked us to wait for you.'

'This is a dream, right?' said Fluke, rubbing his eyes and looking all around, 'but please don't wake me up Tash, I'm really enjoying it.'

'This is no dream, Fluke,' said Elfred, smiling.

'But what's this surrounding us?' asked Tash, pointing all around. 'We couldn't see you a minute ago and now look...' she pointed with her paw at the scene in front of them. 'It's like a large invisible village in the middle of the North Pole,' she said happily.

'Oh, you mean the invisibility shield?' said Elfred. 'Santa had that built many years ago. We have to keep the location of Santa's workshop top secret.'

'But we found you,' said Fluke.

'You were invited, Fluke. Invited by none other than Santa himself,' said Elfred.

'Yes, but *how* did we find you,' asked Tash, 'we didn't have any directions, and all we know is that Santa lives at the North Pole, which is a huge area.'

'You two have the Christmas spirit, Tash. You only have to believe in Christmas and the magic happens. Once you believe, you're able to find us, although the North Pole is a long way to travel for most people,' confirmed Elfred.

'Yeah, and its fr... fr... freezing cold,' shivered Fluke.

'You'll get used to the weather, Fluke. C'mon everyone,' said Elfred, steering Elfonzo and Candysocks back towards the village, 'Santa asked me to take you both over to the dormitory as soon as you arrived, get you cleaned up, and then take you over to his house. I believe one of you requested biscuits? Well, Mrs Claus has been busy baking especially, and they would dearly love to meet you both. Oh, and which one of you has been the slightly naughty one?' asked Elfred with a grin.

Tash chuckled and looked the other way. Fluke just coughed and changed the subject, 'so um err, what's that building over there then?' he asked pointing, 'and that one there?'

'You'll get the tour later with Santa. First to get you cleaned up and then as you'll be working here you've got to meet our *Elf and Safety Officer.*'

'Elf and Safety officer?' chuckled Fluke, grinning from ear to ear.

'We have to run through a few very important rules and regulations before you can work here, things you can and things you can't do,' said Elfred as he shuffled everybody off back into the snowy village.

# The secret set of keys...

It was quiet in this part of the village. A shadowy figure was creeping carefully between the buildings, blending in with the background, careful not to be seen or heard. The only sounds came from its heavy feet crunching the icy snow, but whilst being extra careful, nobody could be completely silent, not in the snow.

The figure scurried from building to building and eventually came to a stop in front of some wooden doors. The secretive figure looked up at the sign hanging above.

WORKSHOP - NO UNAUTHORISED ACCESS

The figure chuckled, 'Pah! No entry? We'll see about that,' and proceeded to fumble with a set of keys. The largest key didn't fit the lock, neither did the second or third. The figure had started to panic that maybe the wrong set of keys had been stolen, when eventually the fourth key fitted, just.

It wasn't a perfect fit by any stretch. The set of keys for the workshop had been stolen a few days ago, and a duplicate set had been hastily cut and filed down, to be used when the time was right. The original keys had been returned before anybody noticed they'd gone. The key cutting took place in a dimly lit back room of a dwelling near the village boundary, an area the villagers called *No Elf's Land*, a small piece of wasteland where nobody lived, well nearly nobody.

The figure enjoyed the solitude of living alone, nobody else visited or lived nearby, but was close enough to make the occasional trip into the village to buy food and provisions. And borrow keys.

The door creaked open and the figure disappeared inside, only to return a few minutes later. Leaving the door unlocked, the figure dashed off. The next building on the list wasn't needed, as it had found what it was looking for.

# Elf and Safety meeting...

'I can't believe we're actually going to meet Santa Claus,' said Tash excitedly. They had been shown to their accommodation, a large dormitory, shared with dozens of other Elves. The room was currently empty. They had been told the Elves were hard at work in the toy workshop. The dorm was a log cabin, snug and heated by a log burning stove positioned in the centre of the room. Rows upon rows of bunkbeds lined each wall.

They left their magic case on the floor in the corner of the room. Sleeping arrangements could be sorted out later and they didn't want to unpack until they knew which of the bunkbeds were for them.

Fluke was stood right beside the stove, rubbing his paws together and holding them out to catch as much of the heat as possible. He turned round to face Tash and began warming his back. 'When do we get to meet Santa Claus, Tash?' he asked excitedly.

'Soon Fluke, very soon. Elfred said he'd be back in a bit, so not long now,' confirmed Tash, looking up to the large clock on the far wall and chuckling. 'Have you seen this clock, Fluke?' asked Tash, 'it's amazing. The biggest and best clock I've ever seen,' she continued. 'Look, they've replaced the twelve numbers with twelve Elves, and have you noticed that every time the minute hand passes an Elf it waves at you, and every hour one of the Elves sings a verse from the twelve days of Christmas. I've never seen anything quite like this in any shop back home,' giggled Tash.

Fluke looked around their new accommodation. 'Toys on every sideboard and table as well, Tash,' he observed.

'They probably try out their new designs, play with them to see whether they work and how much fun they are,' said Tash. 'Also a bit of quality control, Fluke, toys have to be tested before they can be given away as gifts...' Tash stopped speaking as the door opened and in strode Elfred with a pretty female Elf.

'How are you settling in?' asked Elfred, smiling. Turning to Fluke and pointing to the log burning stove, he said, 'and that's an essential piece of equipment up here at the North Pole.' Fluke continued to warm himself. 'This is Holly Wreath, our Elf and Safety officer,' Elfred continued, 'and she has one of the most important jobs here at the workshop.' He said as he guided Holly Wreath over to meet Fluke and Tash.

'Pleased to meet you both,' said Holly in a friendly greeting, who then cleared a table of toys, proceeded to open the file she had been carrying, and took out a sheet of paper and pen. 'I just have to run through some basic rules first, it won't take long though. I know Santa and Mrs Claus are keen to meet you both,' she smiled, adjusted her green Elf hat, looked down the list and began to read.

'Fun – Elves are encouraged to have fun and play pranks whenever possible. The traditional green Elf uniform should be worn whilst at work, and pointy Elf hats are to be worn at all times, except bedtime,' Holly paused to look up and check she wasn't reading too fast and that Fluke and Tash understood. They were nodding and hanging on every word. Satisfied, she carried on.

'The location of Santa's village and workshop is to be kept secret forever. Any broken toys found in the workshop must be repaired before we send them out, and please remember that if you've been feeding or stroking the reindeer, wash your hands. Santa also encourages every Elf to be happy at work, laughing, whistling and singing usually help, and finally, play time! – We recommend half an hour play time mid-morning, one hour after lunch, and a further half an hour play time in the afternoon. I think that just about covers everything,' she turned to Elfred who was happy.

Holly got the pair to sign their names on the dotted line, packed away her paperwork, explained that Fluke and Tash could drop by anytime, if they needed anything, and left the dorm room.

'OK, are you ready?' The pair nodded. Elfred continued, 'I think Santa is keen to see you both now. He wants to give you a tour of the workshop and then get you helping as soon as he feels you're ready. As you probably realise, we're very busy this time of the year and need as much help as possible.' Elfred opened the door and they all stepped outside.

# The village Christmas tree...

The cold air hit them as soon as they stepped outside the dormitory. The warmth from the log burner was becoming a distant memory as they both shivered and trudged through the snow heading towards Santa's house.

'Look Tash, reindeer!' said Fluke in awe, looking over to the stables, stamping his paws trying to keep warm. Sure enough, they saw dozens of young reindeer milling about behind fencing, being fed and exercised.

'They get well looked after here,' said Elfred, 'and probably have better accommodation than us Elves,' he joked. 'That's Santa's house over there, the one with the large chimney,' he pointed, 'Mrs Claus has been baking her extra special biscuits just for you two, so I hope you're peckish.'

'Fluke, hungry?' chuckled Tash, 'is there ever a time when Fluke isn't hungry and thinking about food,' she joked.

The centrepiece of the village was an enormous Christmas tree, which dwarfed all the other trees around the village, and was decked out with a wonderful array of homemade decorations. A team of Elves were busy adding more lights, tinsel and baubles. They were getting the tree ready for the huge celebrations that were held when Santa returned after delivering all the presents.

As they walked past, Fluke couldn't help himself. He stopped and decided to help, well *he thought* he was helping. Studying the tree he moved some baubles and re-arranged some lights. Satisfied, he stood back to admire his handiwork and caught the Chief Tree Decorating Elf staring at him.

'Fluke, this way,' mumbled Elfred, steering Fluke away from the tree. He looked over his shoulder to see the Elves shaking their heads and tutting. 'Sorry about that,' said Elfred apologetically, 'he's new here!' and carted Fluke away before he upset the Elves any more. 'They're very fussy about the tree decorations, Fluke, it's their main job and they don't take too kindly to any of us who get in the way. They've had years at Elf school and have got degrees in tree decorating, even Mr & Mrs Claus don't dare interfere.'

'Come on, Fluke, Santa's house is that large log cabin,' said Tash, as she followed Elfred up the path to the front door.

# Something smells delicious...

They stood under the porch roof and waited patiently on the doorstep for Elfred to knock on Santa's front door. Looking down, Tash noticed they were stood on a large welcome mat, with pictures of reindeer pulling a sledge printed on it. Elfred stood to one side, turned and said, 'do you two want to ring the bell then?'

Looking round for a door knocker or push button doorbell, Tash spotted a length of rope and chuckled. The rope disappeared up into the roof space of the porch.

'What's that stitched on the rope?' said Fluke, stepping closer to get a better view.

'Elves, Fluke,' laughed Tash, 'tiny toy Elves climbing up the rope, look, that one there looks like you Elfred,' said Tash pointing, and they all laughed.

'Try pulling it then,' chuckled Elfred.

Fluke and Tash grabbed hold of the rope and pulled it downwards. As they pulled, little bells on the Elves hats made a quiet jingling sound.

'I feel like one of those bell ringers in church,' chuckled Fluke.

It was a musical doorbell. They heard the magical sound of sleigh bells through the thick wooden door, the bells could be heard ringing throughout Santa's house. The sleigh bells rang for ages until eventually the door was opened and there stood Santa, with Mrs Claus hovering in the background.

'Let them in dearest,' said Mrs Claus drying her hands on a tea towel, 'it's bitterly cold outside,' and she ushered Fluke and Tash into the hallway.

'Welcome to the North Pole,' said Santa jovially. Turning to Elfred he said, 'Thank you Elfred, you can leave our new guests with Mrs Claus and me now.'

Elfred looked to Fluke and Tash and smiled. 'I'll see you both later after Santa has given you the welcome tour,' he said over his shoulder as he shuffled off in the snow, the little bell on his Elf hat jingled as he made his way down the path and back off to work.

Mrs Claus shut the door and draped her arms around the shoulders of Fluke and Tash, steering them through to the living room and a roaring log fire.

'Oh, it's lovely and warm in here,' said Tash, making her way over to the fireplace, rubbing her paws together and enjoying the heat.

Fluke's nose twitched as he smelt wonderful aromas of home baking. 'And something smells delicious,' he said.

'Ho, Ho, Ho,' chuckled Santa, 'that will be Mrs Claus' baking, she's a great cook,' he said and patted his belly, 'we'll have tea and biscuits and then we must get down to some serious work.'

## Bah Humbug

# The Elf that hates Christmas...

**B**ah Humbug, the Elf that loved being naughty, didn't like school, shuddered at the thought of having fun, despised being happy, hated being an Elf, hated Christmas and *really hated* the stupid Elf costumes they all wore, was infamous throughout the Elf academy. Not only had he failed every exam he attempted to take, he was also the only Elf in the whole history of Elf school that had been expelled. Twice!

He was given a second chance and blew it in spectacular style. It wasn't his fault, or maybe it was, he chuckled mischievously to himself, if all the reindeer escaped one night; or all the Christmas lights suddenly stopped working one day; or a whole batch of children's toys in the workshop mysteriously got damaged. That day was fun and he nearly, well almost nearly, smiled when he saw the damage that he had caused.

The distress he put all his teachers through was bad enough, but the head Elf was so upset by Bah Humbug's antics he needed to visit the NES, or *National Elf Service,* and was put on sick leave to recover for a whole two weeks. This caused Santa to expel Bah Humbug for good.

Bah Humbug didn't know why he was like he was. He had tried to fit in at Elf school in the early years, but for some reason he was an outcast. Was he jealous of all the happy Elves? Maybe a little bit, but it was too late now, his latest plan to upset Christmas was well under way. The item he had stolen was inside the large bag he had dragged back through the snow to his dark and gloomy cottage.

The bag was on a large wooden workbench. He undid the draw strings, opened the bag, and peered inside. He chuckled, *Try delivering your presents now Santa,* he thought, *because without this piece of magic equipment, Christmas will have to be cancelled!*

The thought that *little old Bah Humbug,* the outcast Elf that had been expelled for being naughty, held the destiny and fate of Christmas in his hands, did actually make him smile. The first time he had smiled in years, maybe ever. It felt strange, and actually quite nice. Bah Humbug shuddered at the thought. Nice? Happy? *He couldn't possibly be happy*, he thought sadly to himself, *or maybe he could? Maybe, just maybe, he could.*

# The Reindeer stables...

Fluke and Tash tramped through the snow and were led over to the stables. Santa came here every day, sometimes two or three times, to see his beloved reindeer. The heavy wooden doors were opened and they followed Santa inside, glad to be back in the warmth. Fluke shut the door behind them to keep the draft out, turned around and stared in awe. 'Wow! Santa's reindeer,' he whistled and stood gazing around.

The room they entered was huge. Straw was scattered everywhere, giving the place a warm and comforting feeling, the cold wintery weather was forgotten. The reindeer were obviously pleased to see Santa, as one by one they walked over to be petted.

'Dasher, Dancer, how are you two today?' asked Santa, smiling, whilst ruffling the heads of the first two reindeer they came to. 'Prancer, you're looking fit and healthy as always,' he continued, 'Vixen, Comet, Cupid your fur coats are nice and glossy, that reindeer moss and lichen we're feeding you is obviously working wonders, and as for Donner and Blitzen,' Santa continued, 'come here and let me make a fuss of you two as well.'

Santa was surrounded by eight of his herd. He spent a short while with each of his loyal reindeer.

'So where's Randolph?' asked Tash, looking round the barn whilst busily stroking the soft fur of Vixen.

'Over there,' Santa pointed to a figure curled up on the floor at the back of the barn. 'Still feeling a bit under the weather, my old friend?' asked Santa.

'He doesn't look very well, Tash,' said Fluke quietly concerned and watched Santa make his way to the back of the barn. Randolph eventually stood on four wobbly legs and bowed his head to let Santa stroke his fur.

'I hope he's well enough to help pull the sledge,' whispered Tash, 'Christmas is only a week away.'

'I know, without all nine of the reindeer it'll be hard work,' confirmed Fluke.

'Maybe he's caught a cold?' Tash suggested, 'it's freezing up here at the North Pole.'

'A reindeer with a cold?' tittered Fluke, 'Reindeer don't catch colds! Do they?'

'He'll be OK,' muttered Santa with a worried frown, 'a bit tired I expect, with all the extra training they've had.' He turned away, leading Fluke and Tash back out of the barn.

'Training? What training?' asked Tash.

Santa chuckled, 'we have to keep them fit throughout the year,' he indicated with his hand the nine reindeer stood eating and watching. 'Everybody thinks we – and I mean Mrs Claus, the Elves and myself – only work one day a year. It's a full time job, 365 days a year, keeping fit, making toys and delivering all the presents. But I think it's the reindeer that have the hardest job of all, pulling the sledge weighed down with sacks full of presents,' smiled Santa. 'They have a very strict training routine. You'll see them in training a bit later.'

'I suppose people don't realise the work involved,' nodded Tash in agreement.

'I can't wait to see the reindeer down the gym, pumping iron and lifting weights,' chuckled Fluke.

'Enough about all that,' laughed Santa. 'Our worries are over, you're both here to lend a hand,' he rubbed his white beard, deep in thought, 'and to start with, I think we'll introduce you to a day at Elf school. That's where you should start, like every Elf you need to go to school if you want to graduate from the Elf Academy and become a fully-trained and qualified Elf,' and he led them across the yard heading for the school playground.

'School?' groaned Fluke, 'Elves have to go to school?'

'Yes Fluke, even Elves have to go to school, in fact more so than any of us, as they help run the place all year round.'

'What's the matter, Fluke? Don't tell me you've not done your homework? Left your pencil case at home? Not got your PE kit?' Tash laughed and prodded Fluke. 'Come on, it'll be fun, and we might learn something interesting.'

Fluke was steered in the direction of the noisiest building around, a large sign above the entrance read *Welcome to the Elf Academy.*

# Elf School...

Santa opened the main wooden door, passed through the reception area and greeted the two Elves sat at the main desk.

'I'm just showing our two newest recruits around the school,' chuckled Santa, 'can you check to see what lessons we've got arranged for them?'

One of the Elves opened a big book and scanned down the list of names. 'Fluke and Tash, isn't it?' smiled the receptionist, looking up from her book to Tash for confirmation.

'I'm Tash and he's Fluke,' said Tash, pointing to Fluke who was stood gazing around the room.

They were each handed name badges and were asked to clip them to their Elf uniforms.

'OK, so we've got you down...' she scanned the list again, 'for some lessons in *Gift wrapping presents for beginners,* and the always popular *Toy making class.'*

'Toy making? Oh, wow!' said Fluke, 'we'll look forward to that one, won't we Tash?'

'Also we thought it would be good for you to attend our popular *Christmas tree decorating for beginners class,'* the receptionist Elf continued.

'You definitely need the tree decorating class, Fluke,' laughed Tash, and prodded Fluke, 'you've already upset some of the Elves by changing their decorations around when we first got here,'

'I just added the finishing touches to their fine display,' said Fluke with a grin.

The receptionist continued, 'and the *All you need to know about sledge building*, and finally, *Reindeer flying school – lessons for beginners*,' she closed the book, smiled at Fluke and Tash, and looked up to Santa.

'Fantastic,' confirmed Santa, 'You've got a busy day lined up. I'll take you to your first class and come back later to pick you up. Tomorrow, we might let you both loose in our toy workshop!'

'We can't wait, can we Tash?' said Fluke, 'My first day at school, how exciting!'

'Second day at school, Fluke,' whispered Tash.

'Second? When was my first then?'

'Puppy school Fluke, remember? Mum and dad took you to the behaviour class. If I'm not mistaken they didn't take you back, apparently you didn't behave and caused mayhem!'

'Oh yeah, but that doesn't count, it wasn't my fault!' said Fluke, 'I was just so excited to see other dogs I got a bit carried away, that was all,' he muttered, embarrassed, 'it won't happen today, I promise.'

Santa chuckled with his famous *Ho, Ho, Ho* laugh. 'You'll be OK here today. All our teachers are very patient. We've only ever had one pupil expelled from the *Elf Academy*, and I don't intend to have any more.'

Santa led his two new recruits down the long corridor which seemed to go on for ages. They passed loads of classrooms and above each door was a sign indicating which class was inside. A babble of noise could be heard coming from each room. Fluke and Tash peered in through some of the windows as they hurried past, until they finally stopped outside the noisiest room.

Santa confirmed this was their first class of the day, and that the teacher was expecting them. 'This class is always a lively lesson,' chuckled Santa. 'The Elves can be a bit noisy, boisterous, are always getting into mischief, and they like to have lots of fun, so you should enjoy it!'

Tash looked up to the sign that hung above the door.

GIFT WRAPPING PRESENTS FOR BEGINNERS

Fluke moved beside Tash and they both stood on tip-toe and gazed through the window into the classroom, their eyes widened in surprise at the antics taking place.

'What have we let ourselves in for, Tash,' said Fluke, 'I think we're in for an interesting and noisy morning!'

# Farewell North Pole...

**B**ah Humbug took one last look around his tired looking dwelling. *This was meant to be home?* he thought sadly. He'd lived here for many years but it never really felt like home, or as he believed a home should be. He'd heard rumours that other homes were nice, warm, decorated and full of family, where laughter could be heard at meal times. *Pah! Who needs family?*

He'd been OK over the years, living on his own, leading a quiet life in this cold, ramshackle building, nobody to share his house with. No job, well he had had a job once, a basic job, poorly paid he thought, cleaning out the reindeer stables. It was just enough to live on, but he'd been asked to leave for good by Santa, apparently he was a bad influence on all the Elves and reindeer. This was after he'd been expelled from the Elf Academy, so mucking out the stables was the only job he could get, and he couldn't even keep hold of that!

*Well his luck was about to change*, he thought and smiled, slightly. Well a bit. Quite a bit for Bah Humbug, who never smiled. He took one last look inside his bag of possessions. It didn't take long as he didn't have much, his gaze lingered over the one item that would change his life for ever.

Inside the bag, laying at the bottom of the sack, was Santa's magic *time-freezing* machine. This was the one piece of magic equipment that Santa used every year. Fixed to his sledge, it slowed down and froze time, allowing Santa and his reindeer to travel the world delivering presents to all the children on Christmas Eve.

*Well, not this year! Santa will never be able to make his deliveries on time, not without this piece of magic equipment, and it will all be mine now, little old Bah Humbug will be rich! Well, I'll be rich when I manage to sell the gadget to the highest bidder,* he thought.

Bah Humbug had plans, grand plans, to sell this gadget to anybody that could afford it. One of Santa's rivals maybe? He'd heard there were companies in London and New York that competed with Santa every year. Surely one of those companies would be interested in buying this wonderful piece of magic?

They could make a fortune and some of the money would find its way into Bah Humbug's pockets. Well it would have to be his pockets as Bah Humbug didn't have a bank account anymore, his account at the local North Pole branch of the *NEB – National Elf Bank* – had been closed when he was banished to live in the wilderness.

The sack containing all his possessions and the stolen time-freezing machine was slung over his shoulder. Stepping outside his cabin, he closed the door behind him. The air was chilly, and with many miles to cover, he wanted to get going. The weather where he was headed was much warmer. This thought cheered him up, he was tired of being cold all the time. Bah Humbug took his first step towards a new life and headed off into the wilderness, not bothering to turn around, he was a solitary figure striding off, away from the North Pole for good.

# How to gift wrap your teacher...

Tash gingerly opened the classroom door and pushed Fluke through the entrance first, before following close behind. Santa waited outside, told them he'd pick them up after school, and shut the door behind Tash. The noise levels didn't drop at all, if anything the room got noisier. Word had spread that two new students were starting today and the Elves were keen to meet their new classmates.

Fluke tapped Tash on the shoulder and pointed to the front of the class. 'What's that over there?' he asked with a bewildered look on his face.

'Looks like a big bundle of wrapping paper, Fluke,' replied Tash, and then they were both shocked and startled when the big bundle of wrapping paper spoke to them and started to waddle across the floor.

'Welcome! You must be Fluke and Tash, we've been expecting you, haven't we class?' said the mobile mound of paper. A roar of approval went up as the Elves rushed over and surrounded Fluke, Tash and the mysterious bundle of paper.

Upon closer inspection it was now obvious that the bundle of wrapping paper was loosely tied up with multi-coloured ribbons and gift bows. Dozens of gift tags had been stuck randomly, anywhere there was a free space. Both arms struggled and eventually managed to tear through the many layers of gold, red and green paper and offered to shake paws with Fluke and Tash.

'My name's Jinglebella, teacher for the gift wrapping classes,' said a muffled voice behind the wrapping paper. 'Please don't be put off by the rowdy class, it's always fun here, the Elves are just letting off steam, aren't you class?'

'Yes, Jinglebella,' chorused the class together.

'OK class, you've had some fun gift wrapping the teacher,' and then turning to Fluke and Tash she said, 'which by the way isn't normally part of the lesson!' Jinglebella clapped her hands together, smiled and continued, 'now let's get back to our desks and you can show Fluke and Tash what we've learnt this morning,' and the noisy Elves filed back to their desks.

Fluke and Tash picked a row of desks in the middle of the room, next to Elfonzo and his friends, Winterfluff and Fizzylights, and sat down, eager to get started.

Jinglebella broke free from her wrapping paper and stood at the front of the class. She asked one of her Elf assistants, Candysocks, Elfonzo's friend who met Fluke & Tash when they first arrived, to hand out sheets of wrapping paper, bows and plenty of sticky tape. The class sat looking towards the chalkboard. 'OK class, you've got five minutes to create the perfect gift-wrapped, square box. Follow the instructions,' she pointed to the chalkboard, 'and your time starts now!'

The chalkboard had loads of numbered diagrams, a step-by-step guide on how to wrap the perfect present. Each diagram was accompanied by arrows, showing you which way the paper should be folded.

Fluke glanced to the chalkboard and started to read quietly *"Lay your paper out on a flat surface, then place your gift in the centre of the paper. Fold up opposite sides, A and C, and fasten into place with tape. Neatly fold in the edges of the paper and lift up opposite sides B and D, securely sticking them on top of sides A and C...."*

The complicated list of folding and taping instructions went on and on, diagram after diagram, arrows pointing one way, arrows pointing the other, where to place your thumb whilst holding down the paper and where not to place your fingers and thumbs.

It was fair to say that Fluke was getting in a bit of a muddle and struggling to keep up. He glanced down at his best effort and realised that although the box he was meant to be wrapping was a standard square, somehow what he'd created resembled nothing ever seen before. He'd actually designed a brand new shape! He looked over to Tash to see how she was getting on. Not much better was the answer, although her square box was at least sort of box shaped.

'Time up!' hollered Jinglebella and went round the class inspecting the work. 'Not bad Ivycrystals...' she praised one of the Elves, 'keep the edges a bit neater, but overall not bad,' this caused Ivycrystals to glow with pride. Jinglebella went down the line, dishing out praise after praise to her students. 'Well done Winterbaubles, and as for you Twinkletree, you both do listen after all,' she chuckled as Winterbaubles and Twinkletree, both slightly embarrassed at being highly-praised, flushed crimson.

'Oh dear,' said Jinglebella as she stopped at Fluke's desk and held up his work for the class to see. The sight of Fluke's wrapping caused a ripple of laughter from the class. 'It's not quite what we had in mind now, is it Fluke?'

Tash was next in line. 'OK Tash, you can let go of the present,' said Jinglebella.

'Err, I can't,' whispered Tash so the class couldn't hear.

'You can't? Why not?' asked a confused Jinglebella.

'I've stuck my paws to the paper,' said Tash bashfully.

'You've stuck your paws....?' questioned Jinglebella, her voice trailed off as she watched Tash raise both paws in the air, the gift-wrapped box hovered above the desk, well and truly stuck to her paws. Fluke tried to assist and tugged the present free. He then watched in dismay, and the class in amusement, as the paper unfolded itself, leaving Fluke holding the box, whilst the paper drop into a pile on the desk.

'Just as well you two are only here for the morning, as you'd never pass the exams!' chuckled Jinglebella.

The two hours in class whizzed by. Presents after presents were wrapped, different sizes, and difficult shaped gifts were attempted, the longer the class went on the more tricky the presents became to wrap, until Jinglebella finally said, 'OK class, and if you'll pardon the joke, but we'll *wrap* up the lesson for the day, more again tomorrow,' and she began packing up the mess of discarded wrapping paper, sticky tape, bows and ribbon which were scattered everywhere.

# Back to the dorm...

Santa Claus left it until the end of the school day, and as promised, was waiting for them in the corridor. After the Gift wrapping presents for beginners class, Fluke and Tash had followed Elfonzo, Winterfluff, Fizzylights and Candysocks to more lessons which included: Wooden toy making; Christmas tree decorating for beginners; All you need to know about sledge building, and finally, Reindeer flying school – lessons for beginners.

'So how was your day at school?' asked Santa.

'Whoa, what a day! It was great,' said Tash. 'We had basic lessons in sleigh building and an introduction to the reindeer flying school,' she said excitedly.

'Yep, we really enjoyed it Santa, didn't we Tash? Jinglebella said we might have some homework though...' groaned Fluke, 'our first day at school and we've got stuff to revise!'

'I think she was joking Fluke, you've got way too much to do for me,' chuckled Santa, 'as maybe tomorrow or the day after you can help out at the reindeer training school and watch how they learn to fly. It still amazes me after all these years watching them fly,' said Santa, the pride he took in his beloved reindeer was obvious.

'You enjoyed one of the lessons a bit too much Fluke, you nearly got us a detention as well,' chuckled Tash.

'Detention?' said a shocked Santa, 'how?'

'It wasn't my fault,' said Fluke defensively, 'I can't help it if the teacher needs help to decorate the tree properly,' he continued, 'and I only *suggested* that the baubles, tinsel and fairy lights be put in a different place on the tree,' sighed Fluke, looking nervously at Santa.

Santa winced, pulled a funny face, but eventually laughed. 'Fluke, you're going to have to learn that the Elf Christmas Tree Decorators know their stuff and don't take too kindly to being told how to do their job,' he chuckled and led Fluke and Tash back down the corridor.

'Where to next, Santa?' asked Tash, rapidly changing the subject.

'Time for a rest, so back to your dormitory and freshen up. It might be an idea to get to know all the other Elves and then we'll meet in the canteen for evening dinner, lovingly cooked and prepared by our head chef, Nigelfa,' said Santa. Looking around nervously, checking his wife wasn't within earshot, he whispered, 'I have to admit Nigelfa's food is even better than Mrs Claus's cooking, but don't tell her I said that!'

'Oh good, I'm hungry!' said Fluke, licking his lips.

'And tomorrow morning...' continued Santa, also looking forward to sampling Nigelfa's cooking, 'you can pop over to the *Reindeer Flying Academy*, and meet the new herd of reindeer in training.'

'Wow, do we get to fly them in a sleigh?' asked Tash excitedly.

Santa laughed, 'probably not a good idea Tash, they're still learning how to fly, so maybe not just yet!'

'We can help train them though, can't we?' queried Tash.

'Winter Sleigh and Ivy Sleigh will show you around. They'll find you plenty to do, I'm sure. And after you've finished there you can help my dear, old friend, Elfski, in the *Sleigh workshop*. He's putting the final touches to my brand new model, the fastest sleigh I've ever had. This year I'll be using it for the first time, and you two can help him finish it off. It needs to be ready for Christmas Eve, so Elfski is under great pressure to get it finished on time.'

'Wow, sleigh building!' said Tash, and looked over at Fluke who was grinning from ear to ear.

'Oh please, please can we have a go on the sleigh once we've built it?' begged Fluke.

Santa smiled. 'Of course you can! It's essential you learn how to ride one out here in the snow

Fluke, as we don't have any cars or buses, you either walk or use a sleigh.'

# Pranks in the dormitory...

It was agreed they would meet at the canteen in an hour, and for Fluke the hour couldn't come round quick enough as he was famished. They made their way up the path to their dormitory. Tash hesitated, unsure why, but she held back and let Fluke lead the way.

'C'mon slow coach. Let's get inside, warm up, meet the Elves and get ready for dinner,' said Fluke happily. 'What's the matter with you, Tash? Why have you slowed down?'

'It's all a bit too quiet for my liking Fluke,' Tash whispered.

'What do you mean *quiet*? After all the fun and mayhem we've had today I thought you'd like some peace!'

'Look Fluke, you know how mischievous these Elves are, and as we're new here, I just think we ought to be careful,' said Tash.

They reached the top step and Fluke noticed the door was slightly ajar. All was quiet. A light had been left on inside but there were no sounds that any Elves were in.

'Looks like they've gone out for evening dinner and forgotten to shut the door properly,' he tutted and stretched out his paw to push open the door. Stepping inside he said, 'anyway Tash, you're just imagining things, they wouldn't play any tricks on us….' and as he crossed over the threshold, an icy bucket of water, that had been balanced carefully above the door, toppled down soaking a startled Fluke, drenching him from head to paw.

Tash burst out laughing and mimicked Fluke from a couple of seconds before, *'anyway Tash, you're just imagining things, they wouldn't play any tricks on us…'*

'The sneaky, tricky, mischievous little Elves…' said a soaking wet Fluke, standing there whilst a pool of water formed around his paws. 'I bet it was Elfonzo, he seems to be the ringleader.'

'I warned you, Fluke,' chuckled Tash, 'you can always rely on an Elf to be hard working, but never, ever trust an Elf not to play any tricks on you. They're born to play pranks, it's what they do best!' and she sidestepped the puddle and made her way into the room.

Fluke found a towel warming near the log burning stove and dried himself. 'Nice of the Elves to leave a warm towel for me,' he said shaking his head in disbelief, 'and I trusted them, well that'll teach me. I won't fall for that again.'

Tash looked around the vast dormitory. All the beds were empty, but they all appeared to have nameplates at the foot of each bunk. 'Look over here, Fluke,' said Tash and pointed as she walked down the centre of the room, 'all the bunks are taken. Where are we going to sleep?' she queried.

Fluke put the towel back to dry on the log burner and followed Tash. 'I thought cats were meant to have great eyesight?' he asked.

'We do. Why?' replied Tash.

'Not that good though if you missed those!' he laughed and showed Tash a set of large arrows drawn on the floor, pointing to the far end of the dormitory. 'I suggest you eat more carrots Tash, they're meant to help with your eyesight, aren't they?' he joked.

'*More Bunkbeds this way,*' they both read aloud the words written on the floor.

'I guess our accommodation's back there then, Fluke,' whistled Tash. 'Come on, grab the case, we'll find our bunks, unpack and go meet Santa for dinner.'

# Cleaner's cupboard...

Tash strode down to the far end, closely followed by Fluke who was dragging their magic case behind him, studying the nameplates at the foot of each bunk – *Pinecone; Tinsel Socks; Winter Sleigh; Ivy Sleigh; Elfonzo; Snowdrop; Winterfluff; Fizzylights; Candysocks; Fairylights* to name but a few.

'The bunks must be in here,' said Tash, and opened a door to be met by a wall of total darkness.

'Crikey, it's dark in there,' said Fluke and followed Tash inside. The door closed firmly behind them, sealing them inside the darkened room.

'Err, a light switch would be handy right now,' said Tash feeling along the walls, hoping to be able to locate a switch of some kind.

'This brings back memories, Tash,' said Fluke as they bumped into each other.

'Ouch! That was my paw you just trod on,' wailed Tash, 'and what memories?'

'The wardrobe in the Sheriff's room back in Sherwood Forest, pitch black in there, and remember we got stuck until the Nummers rescued us.'

'Oh yeah,' she chuckled, 'I remember that all right. Just as dark in here Fluke, and I can't seem to find a light anywhere,' said Tash. 'Open the case and see if you can find the torch, I know we've got one somewhere.'

Fluke knelt down, opened the case, and luckily found the torch. Switching it on, he shone the beam of light around the room. 'I think we've been stitched up again, Tash,' sighed Fluke. 'This isn't another bedroom with bunkbeds, we're in a cleaner's store cupboard. Look, there's a mop and bucket, a small sink, dishcloths and spare bed linen.'

'Shine the torch towards the door, then we can get out of here,' said Tash and watched as Fluke shone the torch towards the door they entered by.

'Do you see what I see?' asked Fluke stepping towards the door.

'Or don't see...' said Tash, 'they've only gone and taken the handle off the inside. There's no door knob, just a metal spindle. I think we're trapped in here,' said Tash, who yelped again, 'and will you stop treading on my paws!'

Luckily, with a bit of skill, a steady paw and probably more luck than anything, they managed to turn the metal spindle that the door knob was normally fixed to, and escaped back into the main room.

'Right! They want to play tricks on us Tash, so I think it's time to show them who the real experts are when it comes to playing pranks, what do you reckon?'

Tash heartily agreed. They looked around the room, trying to decide what tricks they could play on the Elves. They both thought long and hard and came up with a plan, in fact several plans. Fluke grinned at Tash's suggestions.

They went back into the store cupboard, after firstly wedging the door open. Following some lengthy searching by torchlight, they came back out with a set of screwdrivers, a small hacksaw, a crowbar and a pot of extra strong, quick-setting glue.

To anyone passing by outside, sounds of wood being sawed, screwdrivers being used and lots and lots of giggling could be heard. Thankfully for Fluke and Tash the street was empty. The Elves were in the canteen.

'Revenge will be sweet,' said Fluke, rubbing his paws together in excitement, 'I just hope we're both here to see their faces.' They high-fived each other and set about constructing the traps before rushing out the door to meet Santa and the Elves in the canteen.

# Who's that over there?

The large herd of reindeer were gathered, waiting patiently amongst the fir trees. Cautious of mankind, but normally happy with Elves, reindeer were skittish creatures and were wary of a lot of things, but happily for the two Elves tramping through the snow, they never had any issues or problems whilst seeking out the herd. They were deep in the woods, surrounded by fir trees, doing their daily rounds, when one of the Elves shushed his friend and pointed.

'There, over there,' whispered Winter Sleigh. His colleague, Ivy Sleigh, froze on the spot, not wishing to startle the nervous animals.

'I see them,' Ivy Sleigh whispered back happily, 'there must be about twenty or thirty of them. Ahh, and look, we're privileged today, they've brought their baby calves along with them as well.'

'They look fit and healthy,' confirmed Winter Sleigh, 'this new herd will fit nicely into Santa's reindeer flying school. Talking of Santa...' said Winter Sleigh, walking carefully towards the herd, 'we're showing his two new recruits around the flying school tomorrow.'

'New recruits?' quizzed Ivy Sleigh, 'Oh, *those* new recruits! You mean Fluke and Tash, right? I forgot that Santa's giving them some work experience.'

'We could do with the help, that's for sure,' said Winter Sleigh, and began rummaging in his deep pockets for reindeer treats. Ivy Sleigh searched his pockets as well, and both scattered a special mix of reindeer food onto the snow, watching with delight as the herd got closer, never once showing signs of nerves.

Winter Sleigh and Ivy Sleigh were gladly accepted by the herd. Every reindeer knew these two Elves, as they would soon be trained by them both. Winter Sleigh and Ivy Sleigh ran the Reindeer Flying School for Santa. It was every reindeer's ambition from an early age to be trained, pass the gruelling selection process, hopefully get top marks and one day be selected as part of Santa's Christmas Eve sleigh team.

The pair of Elves were whispering soothing words and patting each and every reindeer in the herd, when without warning the reindeers' ears pricked up. They sensed something approaching and became tense.

Winter Sleigh looked around, wondering what had startled the reindeer, and watched with disappointment as the herd scattered. Ivy Sleigh couldn't hear anything but knew that something had startled the reindeer, when, in the distance, he thought he spied a figure skulking swiftly through the snow.

'Who's that over there?' asked Ivy Sleigh, pointing to where he thought the figure had been.

'I didn't see anybody,' replied Winter Sleigh, 'but you're younger than me and have better eyesight,' he chuckled. 'Let's go and have a look, as I can't think of anybody that would venture this far out of the village.'

'Except us, of course,' laughed Ivy Sleigh.

They shuffled through the snow heading to where Ivy Sleigh thought he'd seen the mysterious figure, and after several minutes of searching, they located a trail of footprints heading off in the distance.

'Shall we follow the trail?' asked Ivy Sleigh.

'No, whoever it was is heading away from the village. Maybe we ought to report this to Santa, as nobody I can think off should be out here, well, except old Bah Humbug. He lives out here somewhere, but surely he'd be heading into the village for supplies? C'mon, let's get back. It's getting late, I'm hungry and we need to get to the canteen, I hear Nigelfa has prepared her speciality dish for tonight's menu,' and they turned back and headed off towards the village.

# Dinner with Santa...

Fluke and Tash left the dormitory and headed over to the canteen. They didn't need to follow the signs, as Fluke's keen sense of smell guided them successfully to the main canteen doors. Hanging around outside, they stood on tip-toes and peered in through a window. Row upon row of benches, full of hungry Elves, greedily devouring big plates of steaming food, were making a babble of noise in between shovelling the food into their mouths.

'Look, there's Santa, sat at the top table,' said Tash and pulled on the door handle to enter the warmth of the canteen.

They spied Elfonzo and Snowdrop sat together. Sat opposite were Fizzylights and Candysocks, all four were in deep conversation. The four Elves looked up as the doors were opened and seemed slightly surprised to see Fluke and Tash stride in.

Tash waved and whispered to Fluke, 'they look shocked to see us so soon, I don't think they were expecting us to get out of the store cupboard as quick as we did. Keep smiling and keep walking,' she said.

'Mrs Claus is sat next to Santa, and there's Elfred as well,' confirmed Fluke, following Tash.

Santa waved, and beckoned them over. 'We've saved you both a seat at the top table,' said Santa happily, indicating two empty chairs. 'Grab a plate from the pile over there,' he pointed to the stack of plates and cutlery, 'join the queue and have Nigelfa serve you, it's delicious...' he felt Mrs Claus staring at him, '...but obviously not as good as yours dearest,' he blushed and patted Mrs Claus's hand reassuringly, 'nothing is as good as your cooking and baking,' he said and turned back to his own dinner.

Tash tittered and shook her head, 'c'mon Fluke, let's see what Nigelfa has cooked,' and grabbed a plate.

Nigelfa was stood behind the counter. Brandishing a large ladle and a massive serving spoon, she smiled as Fluke and Tash came up to the counter.

Fluke was sniffing the air, his nostrils were working overtime as the wonderful smells filled the air. 'Hi Nigelfa, Santa sent us over. Smells lovely, so what do you recommend?' he asked. Studying the choices in front of them, he realised that he didn't recognise anything. 'What's that?' he asked, pointing to a dish.

Nigelfa dug her serving spoon into the bowl that Fluke had been pointing at. 'One of my specialities, Saltfish and carrot stew,' she said and dolloped a huge spoonful on Fluke's plate. Fluke studied it, poked it with his paw and looked at Tash who had her plate ready.

'I do love fish, I really, really, do love fish,' she hummed happily as Nigelfa plopped a spoonful onto Tash's plate.

They made their way back towards the top table, passing Elfonzo's table on the way.

'Err, have you been back to the dormitory yet?' asked Fizzylights, whilst Candysocks looked embarrassed and found something interesting to look at on the other side of the room.

'Yes we have, haven't we Fluke? And very comfy beds they are too,' chuckled Tash.

'It's nice and cozy. What time are you all going back to the rooms?' asked Fluke joining in. 'We'd better follow you back, hadn't we Tash, and get an early night. We can't be late in the morning, Santa wouldn't be too impressed,' he continued.

'No rush, after you finish your dinners,' said Elfonzo, who then watched as Fluke and Tash headed towards Santa's table. The four of them all began whispering at the same time, 'I don't know why the traps didn't work, I thought they'd be stuck in the cupboard for ages and that we'd have to let them out,' Elfonzo continued, shaking his head, mystified.

Dinner with Santa was finished, and they took their empty plates back to Nigelfa. Fluke helped stack them up and offered to carry a pile through to the kitchens, just about managing not to drop anything.

It was agreed. Get a good night's rest, and then early in the morning Fluke and Tash would meet Santa and Mrs Claus, who'd take them over to meet Elfski, the sleigh builder. They said their goodnights, thanked Nigelfa for a lovely dinner and followed Elfonzo and friends out of the door.

# Revenge is sweet...

Elfonzo was chatty as they made their way back to the dormitory. 'So, what do you think of life here in Santa's workshop and our Christmas village?'

'Cold, very, very cold,' shivered Fluke, desperate to get inside and warm himself up in front of the log burning stove. 'It's great though,' he continued between chattering teeth, 'I mean who'd have guessed we would be helping you guys and Santa, I think I'm still dreaming.'

'It's magic, Elfonzo...' agreed Tash, 'a dream come true. We knew you'd be busy here, but I don't think anybody realises how much work there is to do. And as for Elf school, wow, what can I say, it's many years of hard work before you can become a fully trained Elf.'

'About Elf school, I'm confused,' said Fluke, 'you don't seem to attend classes every day, why's that?'

'Its part-time education, Fluke,' said Elfonzo, 'we have school three days a week, learn a lot, have fun, and then for the rest of the week we work in Santa's workshop. Everything we've been taught at school comes in really handy.'

They approached the dormitory. It was quiet and the main lights were off. Just a faint glow from the log burning stove was visible through the windows. Elfonzo followed Fizzylights, Snowdrop and Candysocks up the path. Tash noticed they had slowed down and hesitate as they approached the front door.

'Come on Elfonzo, after you,' chuckled Fluke. 'Why the delay, it's only a door.'

Elfonzo was unusually polite, 'After you Fizzylights, I insist.'

Fizzylights hesitated, fearing the worst he opened the door carefully, and was pleasantly surprised when no bucket of water drenched him.

They filed in, one after the other, with Tash bringing up the rear. Closing the door firmly behind her, she looked down the line of bunk beds and noticed they had all been taken.

Sounds of snoring could be heard coming from most of the bunks as the sleepy Elves rested after a hard day's work.

Fluke and Tash had made comfy beds on the floor, before they'd rushed out to dinner, using two spare mattresses. Tash noticed the small hacksaw and pot of extra strong, quick-setting glue they'd used, poking out from under her bedding. With the Elves tired and getting ready for bed, she quickly lifted the edge of her mattress and hid the evidence, then they both settled down, ready to watch the action unfold.

Elfonzo, Candysocks, Snowdrop and Fizzylights looked at each other, shrugged their shoulders as everything appeared normal and made their way to their respective bunks. Clambering up into the top bunk, Elfonzo laid back and sighed. He loved his bed and was looking forward to a good night's sleep. Suddenly he heard the dreaded sound of wood splintering. His bunk creaked and made a terrible noise as he fell through the wooden slats of his bed, dropped like a stone and landed on the bunk below, which unfortunately was occupied by a sleeping Elf.

Winterfluff woke with a start. The splintering and creaking, plus shouts of panic from Elfonzo above, had Winterfluff fully awake, and he looked up, horrified as Elfonzo came tumbling through the wooden slats and fell into his bunk. The weight of two Elves caused his bunk to break as well, which resulted in a small pile of Elves tangled up on the floor, surrounded by bits of timber from the broken bunkbed.

Fizzylights chuckled at the misfortune his two colleagues had found themselves in, and satisfied his bunk hadn't been tampered with, made his way to the bathroom. 'Would you look at you two...' he laughed, passing Elfonzo and

Winterfluff, 'don't you look nice and cozy...' but was stopped in his tracks as a loose floorboard he'd stepped on sprang up and bopped him in the face.

Candysocks sat up in bed laughing at the scene, 'will you three keep the noise down,' she said between fits of giggles, 'some of us Elves are trying to sleep,' and she took off her pointy Elf hat, swapping it for her nightcap which rested on the bedside table. It suddenly dawned on Candysocks she couldn't remove her hands. They were stuck to her nightcap. She pulled, tugged and did everything she could, but her hands were stuck fast, glued to her nightcap.

Fluke and Tash chuckled to themselves as they watched. 'Don't worry guys,' laughed Fluke, 'the glue only lasts eight hours and wears off.'

'And we'll put the screws back in the floorboards in the morning,' giggled Tash. 'Sleep tight, I know we will, won't we Fluke?'

'OK, OK, we'll call it a draw,' laughed Elfonzo, as Snowdrop, Winterfluff, Fizzylights and Candysocks joined in the fun, 'I think we've met our match with you two!'

# 19th December

# Signpost...

The dormitory was back to normal the next morning. Elfonzo's bed had been repaired by Tash, the glue they'd stuck on the nightcap had worn off and Fluke helped fix the loose floorboards by replacing the screws they'd removed the night before.

Breakfast in the canteen was hastily gobbled down, a hearty dish of Nigelfa's special Christmas porridge which contained oats and berries, all topped with a sprinkling of candy sweets. Elves apparently loved sweet things.

'No school today,' shouted Elfonzo happily, 'we're in the toy workshop all day. Santa has a new batch of children's toys he needs ready for Christmas Eve.'

'We're at the Reindeer Flying Academy this morning, should be exciting,' confirmed Tash.

'We'll see you all later then?' asked Fluke, 'and it's agreed, no pranks on each other today?'

'We're Elves, Fluke, we can't make promises like that!' smiled Candysocks, 'but I think you should be safe...'

'And you'll be safe as well, don't forget,' chuckled Tash.

Candysocks shrieked with laughter. 'Yes, you're right. OK, we'll all be safe as well, it was agreed last night to call it a draw!'

Fluke and Tash grinned and followed as everybody piled out of the canteen. They didn't have much of a choice really, as Nigelfa was keen to clean up the breakfast dishes and all but chased the Elves out, brandishing her trademark large ladle and huge spoon. Most of the Elves were heading towards the large toy workshop, whilst Fluke and Tash stopped to gaze up at the large wooden signpost in the centre of the village, with various arrows pointing in different directions, guiding them to their destination.

'Workshops are over there,' muttered Tash, pointing, trying to get her bearings, 'The Elf school is down that path, Santa's house is back that way,' she indicated over her shoulder with her paw.

'Dormitories are there between those two buildings,' offered Fluke trying to help, pointing in the direction of the arrow.

'Thanks Fluke, I know where the dormitories are, you can see them from here,' laughed Tash and turned back to the signpost. 'The Elf FM radio station is that way, the doctors, or National Elf Service, isn't far away either,' she pointed, 'and yay! The Reindeer Flying Academy is this way,' she added happily, and padded off into the snow. 'C'mon Fluke, keep up and follow the signs, we can't be late, Winter Sleigh and Ivy Sleigh are expecting us.'

'Careful about following the signs, Tash. You know what happened last time we followed some Elf signs,' he chuckled.

'Why, what happened last time?' asked Tash.

'We got locked in a store cupboard, didn't we?' he replied, 'knowing those mischievous Elves, they've probably spun the signs around to send us in the wrong direction!' Tash momentarily slowed down and hesitated.

# Reindeer Flying Academy...

Thankfully, the signpost and arrows hadn't been spun around, and a few minutes later, tramping through the snow and leaving a trail of paw prints behind them, they came across a collection of wooden buildings. A large, open paddock area with fencing around the edge was set to one side, and a more modern looking building which resembled a school, was directly in front of them.

'We've got to get ourselves a sleigh, Tash,' said Fluke slightly out of breath.

'Good idea, I'll sit on it and you can pull me along,' chuckled Tash. 'Well, it looks like we're here, Fluke,' said Tash pointing to a large wooden sign which proudly boasted, "Reindeer Flying Academy", hanging over the entrance to the paddock. A long, winding pathway led right up to the school house.

'Oh, I'm really, really excited, Tash,' said Fluke, eager to get inside and start their day helping train Santa's new herd of trainee reindeer. 'Nobody's going to believe us back home,' he said shaking with joy, 'that we're actually here to help train reindeer for the most important job of the year!' Fluke reached out with his paw, knocked twice and pushed open the front door. They wiped their paws on the mat and entered the office.

'Good morning!' said a muffled voice from underneath a bank of desks. 'I'll be with you in a jiffy, I just need to plug this computer back in and we're good to go!' said the jovial voice.

Fluke looked around the room, his gaze took in a whole bank of computer screens, set up high above a large window which filled the whole width of the room.

Tash wandered over and peered through the glass. 'Wow! Come and take a look, Fluke,' she said and beckoned Fluke over. He stood beside Tash and stared through the glass window in wonderment.

'Impressive, isn't it!' said the voice they had heard a few seconds ago. Turning around they were greeted by a smiling Elf that had obviously finished his job under the desk fixing the computer, and was now stood behind them, his hand extended ready to shake paws. 'Fluke and Tash, I presume? I'm Winter Sleigh, welcome to our Reindeer Flying Academy,' and they shook hands and paws.

'We're happy to be here and help, aren't we Tash?' said Fluke, turning back to gaze through the window. 'So what's happening through there then?' Fluke asked.

'That's Ivy Sleigh out there, checking the equipment,' said Winter Sleigh. Tapping on the glass, he waved, and gave the thumbs up sign to indicate everything was OK. 'We've installed a new piece of training equipment this morning, that's what I was doing under the desk...' confirmed Winter Sleigh, '...fitting a cable from the equipment to these computer screens,' he indicated the bank of computer terminals above the window.

# Treadmill...

They made their way through a couple of doors, and strode out into the large, open arena they had viewed from the opposite side of the window. The room they entered was vast, huge in fact, with a very high ceiling. It needed to be big and reminded Tash of a large gymnasium. The *gymnasium* floor was packed full of exercise machines, each one different, and clearly for performing different tasks.

Striding up to the first piece of equipment, Winter Sleigh explained what it did. 'This...' he said patting the expensive looking bit of kit, 'is a weight and speed sleigh.'

'A what sleigh?' asked Fluke.

'A training sleigh Fluke, it builds up their stamina,' replied Winter Sleigh, and held aloft a large harness, which he passed to Fluke to hold. 'The reindeer stand on the treadmill...' he said, indicating the revolving track, 'we put the harness on them and start the machine, gradually adding more weights and slowly increasing the speed of the running track.'

Ivy Sleigh led in the first of the new trainee recruits. The excited reindeer allowed Fluke to strap the harness on and Fluke then watched as Ivy Sleigh allowed Tash to stand by the control panel, her paw was poised and hovered over the big, green button that had *"Start"* written just below.

Once Winter Sleigh was happy the harness was fitted and the reindeer was comfortable, he nodded to Tash who slammed her paw down and pressed the green start button. Tash joined Fluke at the front of the machine and they both watched in awe as the treadmill sprang to life, the reindeer's legs moved in perfect timing with the speed of the revolving track.

'Fluke, come and turn the speed dial,' instructed Winter Sleigh, pointing to a large knob on the control panel, 'and Tash,' he continued, 'you can turn the dial next to it, that adds more weight to the harness, but turn them both *slowly*,' he said, 'we can't add too much weight or speed all at once!'

Fluke and Tash were now in complete control of the exercise machine, and were offering words of encouragement to the reindeer, words like *"faster, slow coach,"* or *"c'mon, you can do it,"* and *"get those legs pumping."*

Winter Sleigh smiled, happy that his new helpers seemed OK and that the reindeer was responding well to them, and disappeared back into the main control room to fiddle with the computer equipment. He tapped on the glass and indicated for Fluke to gradually increase the speed and for Tash to increase the weight being pulled by the reindeer. He gave a thumbs up sign, indicating the computer was recording all the data from the machine.

Ivy Sleigh lined up the next reindeer for the exercise machine and they went through the same routine, again and again, until eventually all the reindeer had had a go and all the information and data had been recorded, stored and safely logged back in the computer room.

Winter Sleigh popped back into the main arena. 'Onto the next exercise,' he said happily, 'this one's great, you'll love it, I know the reindeer especially enjoy it!'

# The meeting point...

The lonesome figure traipsing through the snow had made steady progress. He was used to hiking, never having owned a sleigh, he'd had to get used to travelling on foot, walking everywhere. He figured there'd be another two days maximum of hard walking before he got to the arranged meeting point.

The Elf community back in the main village thought Bah Humbug was daft and not clever enough to use the internet, but they were wrong, so very wrong. He may not be the brightest Elf around, but he'd secretly learnt how to communicate with the outside world, setting up his small cabin with all the latest radio receivers and computers.

Once he was sure he knew where Santa's time-freezing machine was kept, he had made plans to steal it. He'd then set up his own shop on *elf-Bay* and advertised the gadget for sale to the highest bidder. The number of replies he'd received was staggering. He knew what he had tucked away in his bag was unique, very unique, and, without a doubt, the only one in existence. Some would say the gadget was priceless, so he figured it should sell for a lot of money.

Some email replies he'd received on his *elf mail* account were not very nice. Most people didn't seem to believe that such a machine could actually exist, and they had actually accused him of being a con artist, selling fake products. But it had to exist, how else did Santa get around the world in one night delivering presents to millions of children?

The reply he got from a company in London, SantaToyz Ltd, had made Bah Humbug an incredible offer. They'd arranged to meet him, escort him to the bright city lights of London, put him up in a posh hotel and make him rich, very rich indeed. Of course, the email continued, if the gadget turned out to be fake, the deal would be off and the company wouldn't be happy and would take legal action against Bah Humbug.

They needn't worry. The time-freezing machine was real enough and would make SantaToyz Ltd famous all over the world. '*Move over Santa,*' chuckled Bah Humbug to himself, '*SantaToyz are taking over.*' He carried on hiking, walking as fast as he could, counting down the hours until he'd reach the meeting point.

# The wind tunnel...

The training machine Ivy Sleigh led them to next was completely different from anything that Fluke and Tash had ever seen. It was large, domed in shape and constructed totally of glass. Tash peered inside, confused as to what it was used for. She turned to Fluke, who shrugged his shoulders, as he didn't have a clue what the contraption was either.

'Well, I know what it looks like,' said Fluke, slightly mystified.

'I haven't got a clue, Fluke, so spill the beans, what do you think it is then?' asked Tash.

'A snow dome or snow globe!' he laughed.

'Snow dome?' Tash giggled, 'what, those little glass domes with a Christmas village scene, filled full of water and snowflakes appear when you pick it up and shake it?'

'I said it *looked* like one, I didn't say it was one!' Fluke laughed again and waited patiently for Ivy Sleigh to explain what they were actually looking at.

'Welcome to our very own wind tunnel machine,' said Ivy Sleigh, and chuckled at the faces both Fluke and Tash were pulling.

'Wow, a wind tunnel machine, but why? What's it used for exactly?' asked Tash peering through the glass.

'It gives the trainee reindeer recruits their first experience of flying,' replied Ivy Sleigh, 'even the experienced reindeer use it to practice.'

'Cool!' exclaimed Fluke, who was getting very excited at the prospect of watching some sky diving reindeer.

'Cool indeed...' chuckled Ivy Sleigh, 'we actually set the temperature inside the dome to match the freezing cold artic weather they'll be flying in.'

'Yep, we can confirm how chilly it is outside,' confirmed Tash, 'my goggles iced up when we flew here on our magic case!'

Ivy Sleigh laughed and said, 'the wind tunnel also helps the reindeer practice flying in very windy conditions, so when they're pulling the sleigh they don't get blown off course. It helps improve their balancing technique, but most of all, we use it because it's great fun!'

# Sky diving dalmatian...

'Oh, please, please, please can I have a go?' begged Fluke. 'I promise I won't break anything, and I won't touch any buttons that I'm not supposed to touch!'

'Well, seeing as you do some flying on your magic case, it might be a good idea for you to learn the basics,' said Ivy Sleigh. 'Come on then Fluke, follow me, and we'll get you fitted out with the safety goggles and crash helmet. You'll have to wear these or I'll be in trouble with our Elf and Safety Officer.'

'Oh, we've already met Holly Wreath,' said Fluke, 'she's lovely, but strict, so we better stick to the rules!' and followed Ivy Sleigh to the changing room to get kitted out.

Fluke returned several minutes later. Tash couldn't help but laugh as Ivy Sleigh led Fluke up to the glass dome. He wore a thick padded jacket, safety crash helmet, gloves, scarf, and safety goggles. A door was opened in the dome, and after some brief safety checks and some last minute advice from Ivy Sleigh, Fluke stood in the centre of the dome, waiting patiently. Ivy Sleigh closed the door firmly, and strode over to Tash, who was waiting patiently at the control panel.

'OK, Tash,' said Ivy Sleigh, 'you can start the machine by pressing that button,' he pointed to a green start button, 'and when I tell you to, you can turn this large dial,' said Ivy Sleigh, pointing to a knob which had "Slow" on the left hand side and "Fast" written to the right.

Tash pressed the button as instructed and heard the wind turbines starting up. She peered through the glass dome, watching in fascination as Fluke's ears began to flap underneath his crash helmet. His scarf came untucked, flapping in the wind, and his face wrinkled as a blast of icy cold air began to fill the glass chamber.

'I've got to pop back to the control room...' said Ivy Sleigh pointing over his shoulder, 'to make sure the computers are recording all the data from the wind machine. When I give the sign, slowly, and I mean *very slowly*, turn the wind speed dial, steadily increasing the wind speed. I'll be back in a few minutes to check on you both.'

Tash watched as Ivy Sleigh disappeared. She chuckled to herself, determined to have some fun at Fluke's expense. She smiled as her paw hovered over the speed dial. Fluke gave her a thumbs up sign, clearly enjoying his experience so far. With a wicked grin, Tash turned the dial slowly to the right and heard the change in the turbines as the wind speed picked up. Fluke looked surprised as he lifted off the floor, his legs and paws flapping as he tried to control himself. He was saying something, but due to the thickness of the glass, Tash couldn't hear what he was saying.

'What was that, Fluke?' said Tash laughing, watching Fluke hover in the air, 'you want to go faster?' And turned the dial even further.

Fluke started panicking. His paws were flapping faster and faster as he began to fly around the dome. He was desperately trying to reach the door, but as the wind speed increased even further, he started to perform somersaults. Now somersaults would have been great, and a real showstopper, if only he'd actually meant to perform these acrobatics, but sadly for Fluke, and happily for Tash, *she* was in control and turned the dial even further.

As Tash turned the dial to maximum speed, Fluke began whizzing around the inside edge of the dome. Every time he flew past Tash, he was spinning head over paw, bouncing off the glass walls, but his padded jacket and safety helmet helped to prevent any damage. Tash heard Ivy Sleigh heading back, so turned the wind speed dial back to minimum. She watched as Fluke stopped his spinning and whizzing, and slid down the glass wall directly in front of the control panel where Tash was stood.

'I forgot my clipboard and notebook,' said Ivy Sleigh and glanced inside the now empty dome. Fluke had found the door handle, letting himself out, he flopped to the floor, exhausted. 'Ready when you are, Fluke,' said Ivy Sleigh and watched as Fluke stood unsteadily on his paws, and leant against the glass. 'You look a bit pale, Fluke, is everything OK? Are you feeling ill?' asked Ivy Sleigh, slightly concerned.

'I don't think wind tunnels and skydiving are for me,' said Fluke, and on unsteady paws, his head still spinning, he wobbled dizzily back towards the changing room.

# SantaToyz Ltd...

**B**ah Humbug approached the meeting point carefully. He was wary, and a little bit nervous. The meeting had been arranged on his elf Mail account, and the message had said that SantaToyz Ltd would send some representatives to take him to London to discuss the sale of the time-freezing machine. It was natural, he guessed, that their experts would want to examine the machine before they handed over any money.

Bah Humbug had got to the meeting point a bit early so he could scout around, find a safe place to watch from and see who turned up. He pitched up a windproof tent, white in colour, so it blended in with the surrounding snow, and waited patiently.

It was cosy in his tent and he was worn out after such a long walk so he dozed off, but was rudely awoken by the noise of a strange sounding engine approaching. A large hovercraft, with the logo "SantaToyz Ltd" written down the side, appeared over the horizon, skimming across the snowy landscape. It pulled up, the engines were stopped and then there was silence. Four men jumped from the strange looking craft and leapt onto the snow.

Bah Humbug watched the four men stamping their feet and blowing on their hands to warm up. They kept checking their watches and, after several minutes, they were about to jump back aboard their craft and leave when Bah Humbug left his tent. Clutching his bag which contained the time-freezing gadget, he walked over to the craft and greeted the men. A lot of handshakes were exchanged and Bah Humbug was invited to board the hovercraft.

The engines were started, the craft spun around and headed off, taking Bah Humbug to an airport and a new life in the city. Destination – London.

# We're going to the cinema...

'How's your head, Fluke?' laughed Tash as they left the changing rooms and followed Ivy Sleigh to the next training machine.

'Still spinning!' exclaimed Fluke.

'The machine must be faulty, Fluke, I don't know what happened, honest! All I did was turn the dial a little, tiny bit and it got stuck on full power,' she said slyly, trying to keep a straight face and not burst out laughing.

'Yeah, whatever! So what's next?' asked Fluke, changing the subject. 'Which machine are we looking at now?' He said as they stopped, and studied the new piece of equipment.

'Looks like a sleigh, harness and cinema screen' said Tash, looking towards Ivy Sleigh for confirmation.

'Yay! We're going to the pictures to watch a movie!' said Fluke happily. 'Where's the popcorn?' he laughed.

'No Fluke, we're not going to the cinema,' laughed Ivy Sleigh, shaking his head. 'It is, however, a sleigh, well kind of,' he continued. 'It's actually a flight simulator, the best one in the world by a long way. Our reindeer strap on the harness and stand on this special movable floor,' he indicated with a sweep of his hand, 'which has sensors built in. When the reindeer move, so does the picture on the big projector screen. It's very lifelike, and after the wind tunnel experience it prepares them for some actual flying.'

They saw Winter Sleigh leading some young reindeer across the floor, heading towards the simulator. 'I hear your first experience in the wind tunnel didn't go according to plan, Fluke,' he said chuckling, 'maybe a ride in the simulator machine will be more suitable?'

'Oh, yes please, can we both have a go?' asked Tash.

'Strap yourselves into the sleigh then,' instructed Winter Sleigh, 'and Ivy Sleigh will fasten the reindeer into the harness,' he said and watched as Tash jumped in the sleigh first, closely followed by Fluke.

'Which screen do you want?' asked Ivy Sleigh as he scrolled through hundreds of options.

'Screen? What do you mean, which screen do we want?' asked Tash.

'You can pick a country, a city or anywhere in the world to fly around. Don't forget Santa delivers presents to *everybody* in every country, so we've updated the projector machine to include every country, every city, every street and even every house.'

'Wow, that's awesome!' said Fluke and turned to Tash. 'Where to, captain?' he asked.

Tash thought long and hard. 'New York, Washington, Paris and London,' said Tash and waited whilst Ivy Sleigh set the program on the machine.

They were all set. Seat belts were fastened securely. Winter Sleigh flicked switches, set dials and his hand hovered above the green start button. 'Ready?' he asked.

'We're ready,' said Fluke, 'New York here we come!' And he checked his seat belt one more time.

The big screen in front of them burst into life.

# New York, Washington, Paris and London...

It was just like being at a cinema, with front row seats. The image on the screen was so clear and there was even sound coming from some hidden speakers. The lights in the training complex were dimmed, throwing the whole gymnasium into near darkness, which kind of made sense really, as Santa flew through the night on Christmas Eve.

The reindeer were pulling the sledge on the screen, firstly leaning left and then steering right. The sleigh they were in also moved, and tilted at exactly the same time as the reindeer. Tash had hold of the reins, and with a gentle pull she began to steer the reindeer. They were flying over the East river, and heading towards a large bridge.

'Is that the Brooklyn Bridge?' asked Tash.

'I think so,' said Fluke, who promptly ducked and lifted his paws up as Tash steered them underneath the bridge, skimming them inches above the water.

'Why did you duck and lift your paws?' asked Tash, laughing.

'If feels so real, like we're actually in New York,' gasped Fluke, 'I thought I might get my paws wet we were so close to the water!' They began to fly down Broadway, and then headed off to Wall Street, 'Will you keep your eyes on the road, you nearly crashed into a yellow taxi cab!'

After successfully navigating Wall Street, they headed off to the capital, Washington. 'The White House? Seriously? You mean Santa even delivers presents to the President of America?' laughed Tash, watching the big screen and letting the reindeer pull them along.

'Only if he's been good and is on Santa's nice list!' said Winter Sleigh joining in the fun.

Next on the list was Paris. They had approached the Eiffel tower a bit too quickly, causing Fluke to shut his eyes, flew around the base of the Tower, and under the magnificent arch. The reindeer weren't fazed at all and steered them through and off to safety.

They headed off over the English Channel, flying above the famous White Cliffs of Dover, and then onwards to London. The bright city lights were dazzling as they flew first down a packed Oxford Street, then Regent Street, around Big Ben, which just happened to chime as they flew around the top, and finally over Buckingham Palace.

'I wonder what Santa gives the Queen for Christmas,' said Fluke.

'That's top secret. Santa won't give anybody that information,' said Winter Sleigh and he reached over to turn off the machine.

Their eventful day had come to an end. They thanked Winter Sleigh and Ivy Sleigh for looking after them.

'Thanks guys, that was amazing,' said Tash. They stroked the reindeer and headed out of the training complex.

'I don't think people appreciate how much work goes into running this place,' said Fluke, 'and I don't just mean the training centre, I mean the whole of Santa's workshop village. There's so much going on every day, not just the one day a year that we're all used to.'

'Your right there, Fluke,' agreed Tash. 'Hungry yet?' she asked and watched Fluke's eyes light up. 'We'd best go and see what Nigelfa has been cooking today, hadn't we,' and they raced each other to the canteen to meet up with the Elfonzo and the rest of the hard working Elves.

## 20th December

# Sleigh bells...

Evening dinner had been eaten by the hungry Elves, and both Fluke and Tash managed to polish off a bowl of Nigelfa's home cooking. Satisfied, and very full, they had a quiet night back in the dormitory. No tricks or pranks for anybody to worry about this time around.

Morning came around quickly, and whilst the Elves went to the workshop for another busy day, Fluke and Tash traipsed through the snow to Santa's house. He was taking them to visit Elfski, the Sleigh Builder.

Making their way out of the village, the three of them headed down a snowy footpath. Several minutes later they came across a small wooden building with a wonky front door, partly open. Santa pulled the handle, they stepped over the threshold, and found an Elf slumped over a writing desk studying some design drawings and muttering to himself.

'Ahh, Elfski,' said Santa gleefully, 'You're in! I've managed to find you some little helpers.'

The Elf sat upright, turned around and greeted Santa, 'Oh at last!' he joked and greeted his new guests, shaking paws with Fluke and Tash.

'So you're Santa's Sleigh Builder then?' asked Fluke, studying the bits of paper and drawings that filled Elfski's desk.

'I certainly am, and I've designed a brand new sleigh for Santa. It's almost finished and just needs testing,' said Elfski, who made his way over to a canvas cover that was hiding something bulky underneath. 'This is the first time anybody has seen my new design,' he looked towards Santa, 'it's bigger, faster, and has all the latest gadgets you requested, and gives you more room for all those presents.' He dramatically pulled the canvas away revealing a brand new, shiny sleigh.

'Very impressive, and look...' Santa walked over to inspect his new sleigh, 'more leg room,' he pointed, 'and I love the new paint finish, as well.'

'OK, you two...' said Elfski, handing Tash a cloth and Fluke a pot of wax, 'if you want to help, you can start by waxing and polishing the new sleigh. We can't have it looking dirty when Santa uses it for the first time, now can we?'

'I'll leave you to help Elfski,' said Santa, stepping back outside, 'oh, and Elfski, after they've finished here, if you could lend Fluke and Tash a small sleigh and send them over to Pinecone's workshop to inspect the Christmas Tree farm, but make sure they don't get lost.'

It was back-breaking work, but several coats of wax and several polishes later, the work was finished.

Standing back to admire their handiwork, Fluke said, 'you can see our reflections in the bodywork Tash, it's that shiny.'

Elfski was working on another, smaller sleigh. He looked up, smiled, and said, 'good work you two. You can fit the sleigh bells now, that's the last, well almost the last item to be added.' He got up and walked over to a large cupboard, the word "accessories" was painted on the front.

Opening the doors, he rummaged around and picked out two large sets of bells, fixed to long leather straps. He handed a set to Fluke and a set to Tash, then watched as they fixed the leather straps onto little hooks which ran down both sides of the sleigh.

'Finished!' said Fluke

'Nearly, Fluke,' laughed Elfski, 'just one more item to add, and without a doubt the most important gadget of all!'

# Dashboard controls...

Whilst Elfski walked over to another cupboard marked "Special Gadgets", Tash looked into the sleigh and gazed at the dashboard. 'What do all these lights, switches and dials do then, Elfski?' she asked, mystified.

'Oh, they're all gadgets that Santa has had designed and installed over the years,' said Elfski over his shoulder, as he rummaged around in individual boxes, 'it makes navigating his sleigh around the world a lot easier.'

'So what does this button do?' asked Fluke, and without asking permission he pressed a green button and watched in fascination as a mini TV screen set in the dashboard blinked into life.

Turning around, Elfski looked over, chuckled, and said, 'that one is the GPS navigation system, or satnav. It's got every address in the world stored in its memory, and helps Santa with all those difficult, hard to find homes.'

'And this one?' queried Fluke, pressing a blue button. A low hum could be heard from the dashboard as whatever Fluke had pressed

warmed up, filling the cockpit with a pale blue light.

'It's a weather map, Fluke,' said Elfski, as he turned back to his search, 'it gives a live report on weather conditions. You know, like where in the world it's currently snowing, or when a blizzard is forecast, if any fog is due, where any storm or high winds are, if any rain is forecast, that type of thing,' Elfski continued, 'it's operated from the Elf HQ – Traffic and Weather Centre.'

Several more buttons were pressed and switches flicked by an eager Fluke. Buttons and switches which controlled a whole manner of gizmos and gadgets, such as a naughty or nice sensor; present counter; next child on the list button; speedometer; altitude level sensor; radar screen; reindeer energy level monitor; hot drinks dispenser; side, rear and underneath parking sensors, and rear driving camera.

Fluke pressed another button. It was red and had "warning" in big, bold letters stamped on it. A loud bell could be heard coming from the dashboard. It filled Elfski's workshop with a deafening sound. Fluke tried to turn off the noise by repeatedly pressing the button again 'What was that button for?' he breathed a huge sigh of relief now the warning bell had finally been silenced.

Elfski laughed, 'Santa had that fitted on one of his old sleighs a couple of years ago. It's a Traffic Warden sensor.'

'Traffic Warden sensor?' asked Fluke.

'Santa got a parking ticket a few years ago. It was late at night, obviously...' said Elfski, 'he'd left his sleigh beside the road in a no parking zone whilst he popped into a row of houses to deliver some presents. When he came back out, he had a parking ticket and they'd tried to fix a wheel clamp to the sleigh runners!' laughed Elfski.

'Seriously? Santa got a parking ticket? Did he pay the fine?' laughed Tash.

'Oh yes,' confirmed Elfski, 'he paid alright, Mrs Claus was furious with him! Then after we all teased him about it, he designed the warning bell, it lets him know if there's any traffic wardens nearby!'

Tash wanted a go at pressing buttons. She leant in and began pressing more switches, tapping dials and then jumped back, startled, as music blared from some hidden speakers set in the dash and floor.

'You've found the music station then,' said Elfski. 'Our very own radio station, Elf FM,' he laughed, 'I just wish that I could find the one item we need to make the sleigh work,' he mumbled to himself.

'Santa's workshop village has its own radio station?' asked a bewildered Tash.

'It certainly does, Tash,' said Elfski, 'we love music up here. We have our very own resident DJ called Elfis,...' He abruptly stopped talking, removed his Elf hat, scratched his head and turned around. His face had gone pale and he looked worried. Very worried indeed. 'Santa's in trouble. Big, big trouble. It's gone!'

# Emergency meeting...

The canteen was full to the brim with worried-looking Elves pacing up and down.

'Christmas is going to be cancelled?' asked a stunned Tash, turning to Elfonzo for confirmation. Word and rumours were spreading rapidly throughout the village, as more and more Elves crammed into the already overflowing room.

Once Elfski had noticed the missing time-freezing machine, they had rushed back to inform Santa of this distressing news, who then promptly called an emergency meeting, which was to be held at 1pm.

Elfonzo shrugged his shoulders, 'I don't see how Christmas can carry on if Santa can't deliver his presents.'

'But it's Christmas, it can't be cancelled. Can it?' said Fluke.

'So who do you think has stolen the time-freezing machine?' asked Tash, and watched as Candysocks, Fizzylights and Winterfluff all shook their heads in disbelief.

'That's why we're here, Tash,' said a sad-looking Winterfluff, 'to try and work out who could be so nasty to ruin Christmas for everybody.'

A hush fell across the room as Santa stood on the small stage that had been rapidly set up. He gazed around the room and started to speak. 'For the first time in all my years, and there's been plenty let me tell you, Christmas is on the verge of being cancelled.' Santa stopped for a few seconds to compose himself. Mrs Claus patted him on his back and took hold of his hand. This small gesture spurred Santa on, and he continued. 'If anybody has news about the missing time-freezing machine, then now is the time to share the information,' he said, looking hopefully around the room.

A hesitant arm was raised from the middle of the packed room. 'Yes Winter Sleigh, you have some news?' said Santa, hopefully.

'I'm not sure, Santa,' said Winter Sleigh hesitantly.

'Well, some news is better than none, so what is it you want to say?' said Santa.

'Well, Ivy Sleigh and I were out tending to the wild reindeer, you know as we do every day, when the herd were startled by something. Ivy Sleigh here...' he indicated his colleague, 'is younger than me and has better eyesight. He thought he saw a hunched figure in the distance heading away from the village.'

'Is this true?' asked Santa kindly, encouraging Ivy Sleigh to speak up.

'Yes Santa, I've been wracking my brains as to who it may have been. I mean, nobody heads out of the village and into the wastelands, especially on their own, and the only Elf I know that lives out in the wilderness is old Bah Humbug...' He was stopped midsentence by Santa.

'Of course! Bah Humbug! I might have known that one day he'd turn completely bad. He hates Christmas, hates being an Elf, and he doesn't like me too much either since I expelled him all those years ago from Elf School,' said Santa, deep in thought.

Fluke raised a paw, and waited for Santa to spot him in the crowd. 'Yes Fluke, you have a question?' said Santa.

'Why don't we visit Bah Humbug's place and see if there's any clues as to where he went?' said Fluke.

'Good idea,' agreed Santa, 'we might catch him with the machine, or at least find some clues as to what he's done with it.' A search party was rapidly organised. The group, which consisted of Santa, Fluke, Tash, Winter Sleigh and Ivy Sleigh, started to head out to the wasteland that Bah Humbug had called home. Elfonzo, Snowdrop, Winterfluff, Fizzylights and Candysocks begged to tag along as well. They'd argued that as they are always playing out in the wilderness they might know of any special, hard to find places Bah Humbug might be hiding, or could possibly have stashed the stolen time-freezing machine. Santa agreed and the extra Elves joined the search party, well this was an emergency after all.

# What a dump...

The group silently approached the run down dwelling that was once the home of Bah Humbug. Fluke crept up the path towards the front door, the rest of the party following close behind. He noticed the door was slightly ajar, and carefully, with his paw, he pushed the squeaky wooden door wide open and stepped backwards quickly, covering his head with both paws.

'Are you OK, Fluke?' asked Santa, wondering why Fluke had leapt backwards whilst opening the door.

'Oh, it's just a habit I've recently developed since sleeping in the dormitory. You can't be too careful when opening doors around here, can you Elfonzo?' he said, gazing towards the young Elves, who promptly began chuckling amongst themselves.

Tash moved Fluke out of the way and entered the gloomy interior, firstly checking that no surprise buckets or trip wires had been set. The interior was silent. She pulled out her torch and flicked on the switch. The beam of light moved around the room, penetrating the darkness. 'What a dump!' she whispered and moved forwards, stepping over discarded furniture that was scattered everywhere.

It was basically a single room with a small bed in one corner, some basic cooking equipment, a couple of wall units for storing supplies and a rocking chair next to a log burning stove. Reaching out to touch the surface, Elfonzo shivered as his hand touched the cold metal. 'The log burner hasn't been used in a while, it's stone cold,' he confirmed and blew on his hands to warm them up.

'Looks like he packed in a hurry, and is not in any rush to return either,' said Fluke, stepping alongside Tash. 'Do you guys notice anything strange?' he said gazing around. 'The whole room is in a complete mess, furniture turned upside down, cutlery left on the side, everything except the bed.'

'What do you mean?' queried Santa.

'Everything is in complete disarray, messy and untidy, all apart from the bed. Look, it's perfectly tidy, freshly made, almost like it's just recently been pulled back into place. Its hiding something, I'm sure it is.'

The bed was dragged away from the wall, revealing a rug covering the floor where the bed had been. 'What's it being used to cover then?' said Fluke, kneeling down. Grabbing hold of one corner, he pulled the rug away to reveal what looked like a trap door in the floor.

Tash whistled and said, 'well, what do we have here then? A secret trap door, but a door leading to what, I wonder? C'mon Fluke, let's get the trap door open and see what's inside.' She knelt down alongside Fluke, helping lift the heavy wooden trap door to reveal a set of steps leading down into a dark, dingy and musty smelling room.

# The secret basement...

Tash led the way; creeping hesitantly down the creaky wooden stairs, her torch shining brightly, its beam of light trying to penetrate the darkness down below. Fluke, Santa and the rest followed carefully, watching their footsteps, not wanting to take a tumble.

Fluke jumped out of his skin as he walked straight into a large cobweb, which completely covered his face. 'Yuk, cobwebs, I've got a mouthful of web, how come you missed walking straight through it, Tash?' whispered Fluke.

'Ha-ha, for once it pays to be shorter than you! I must have walked underneath it,' she chuckled.

They filed into a single room and gazed around the basement. Tash spotted an oil-filled lantern hanging from a hook on the wall and lit it, the room was suddenly flooded with bright light.

'OK, so we have a desk, a computer, and a set of maps on the wall,' said Tash walking over to the desk, 'and the red power light for the computer is on, Bah Humbug must have forgotten to switch it off.'

'Turn on the computer screen, Tash,' urged Elfonzo, 'let's see what Bah Humbug was looking at.'

Tash obliged, pressing the On button and moving the mouse. They all gathered around the computer screen and watched in fascination as the screen swam into life.

'Drat! The computer wants a password to let us get in. Any ideas?' asked Tash, turning around to speak to Santa.

Santa tugged at his white beard and thought long and hard. 'Well, knowing old Bah Humbug like I do, try typing "I HATE CHRISTMAS" as a password.

Tash flexed her paws, and began typing the password Santa had given her. She clicked the OK button and waited for the computer. 'Yes! It's worked, the computer's let us in, now to find out what Bah Humbug's been looking at, hopefully it will give us some clues as to where he's gone.'

Tash opened different folders on the computer's desktop, and clicked Bah Humbug's elf mail account. They all gathered as close to the screen as possible, watching as Tash opened different elf mails, until the final one was opened. A gasp went around the room as it became obvious what Bah Humbug had done.

'Err, Santa, it looks like Bah Humbug has sold it,' said Tash reading the elf mail one more time.

'He's done what? He's sold our time-freezing machine?' said Santa, shaking his head in utter disbelief, and moving closer to the screen. He popped on a pair of reading glasses and began to read the elf mail for himself, just to make sure he hadn't misheard Tash.

'Looks like he sold it on elfBay,' said Tash, scrolling down the screen, 'to a company called SantaToyz Ltd in London, for a huge amount of money. Bah Humbug was due to meet the company representatives nearby at a meeting point, and then it looks like they were taking him back to a posh London hotel to complete the sale.' Tash sighed.

'Well, that's it then,' said Santa sadly, 'Christmas is cancelled. I can't deliver the presents in one night without the time-freezing machine, it's just impossible.'

'Now what do we do?' said Elfonzo, 'all those excited children are going to be so upset.'

'We'll have to contact the TV news channels, the newspapers and anybody else we can think of. It's a horrid thought, but there's nothing else we can do. SantaToyz Ltd will take over, Bah Humbug has beaten us, after all these years he's now got his revenge,' said Santa, turning away from the computer screen.

Fluke coughed to get everybody's attention. 'Err, maybe I'm missing something here guys, but why don't we go and get it back?' he said, looking at the group.

'How? London's a big place Fluke, I should know, I deliver there every year, or *did* deliver, sadly not any more though,' replied Santa.

'Fluke's right, Santa,' said Tash, 'look at the screen again. Bah Humbug has a confirmed booking form for the hotel…' and she studied the screen, 'the hotel's called *The Ritz*, and we've even got the room number – room 301.'

'Surely we're too late?' queried Santa. 'Without my time-freezing machine it'll take me days to get there, and if anybody sees me out in the sleigh before Christmas it will be all over the news channels and newspapers.'

'We'll go to London, find the hotel and bring back the time-freezing machine,' offered Tash. 'With our magic suitcase we'll be there in a few minutes.'

'Well, what are we waiting for?' said Fluke, 'We now know where we're going, so let's go!'

## 21<sup>st</sup> December

# A trip to London...

Tash dragged their magic case out, and was instantly surrounded by Santa and his Elves, watching in fascinated silence. She busied herself setting the co-ordinates. Elfonzo was anxious to accompany Fluke and Tash in their desperate search for Santa's missing machine. He argued it would be a good idea for them to have some back up, just in case, as it might be dangerous, and nobody knew what to expect when they got to London. They were dealing with criminals after all.

A strong friendship had built up between Fluke, Tash and the Elves, so it was an easy choice to agree that Elfonzo could come with them, as long as Santa was OK with it. He was.

Fluke and Tash sat patiently on the magic suitcase, waiting for Elfonzo. He'd rushed out of the dormitory a couple of minutes before, shouting, 'wait there, don't go without me, I'll be back in a minute.'

Santa shrugged his shoulders and looked as confused as everybody, as they all watched Elfonzo run out the door.

'What's Elfonzo up to?' muttered Tash, keen and eager to be off. Turning to Santa, she said, 'we'll rescue your time-freezing machine Santa, don't you worry, well, we will as soon as Elfonzo hurries up. Where is he?'

The dormitory door was flung wide open and a breathless Elfonzo came charging back into the room, a bag slung over his shoulder. 'Right, what are we all waiting for, shall we go then?' And he jumped onto the magic case, settled in behind Tash, who was upfront, and in front of Fluke who was, as usual, sat at the back.

'Hold on tight, Elfonzo...' warned Fluke, 'because if you'd seen Tash's driving earlier on the flight simulator you might not have been in so much of a hurry to fly with us,' he joked.

Tash turned the handle three times. The magic case started spinning, Fluke's ears began to flap and the magic case promptly disappeared from the dormitory.

Santa and the Elves stared in disbelief at the empty spot where seconds ago a magic suitcase had been sat. Santa poked the floor with his foot, just wanting to confirm it had actually disappeared. Turning to one of his Elves, and slightly jealous that he didn't have a magic time travelling suitcase himself, he chuckled, 'so how come you haven't designed me one of these yet?'

# Room service...

$\mathcal{B}$ ah Humbug sat in his hotel room, and not for the first time since he'd arrived he was thinking how lucky he was. His luck had changed for the better, of that he was certain. Room 301, the penthouse suite, and his for the next two nights, was massive. Even the bathroom was enormous and very, very posh. It certainly beat living in a cold, dark and damp cottage back at the North Pole.

He was hungry, and after studying the menu for a few minutes, he decided it was time to order some room service. He wanted to have his food delivered by waiters, just like in the movies. He phoned down to reception and ordered everything on the menu, well, he wasn't paying for it after all. SantaToyz Ltd were paying for everything – the room, his dinners, his transport – and as the meeting with their top bosses wasn't until later tonight, he figured he had time for dinner and a hot soak in the bath.

His mind briefly wandered back to his old life, the miserable life he had left behind, and wondered if Santa had discovered that his gadget had gone missing yet. Well, it was nearly Christmas, only a few days to go, and soon Bah Humbug would be the richest Elf in history, and SantaToyz Ltd would be one of the richest companies in the world.

# Hotel reception...

The magic case materialised from thin air directly into the hotel lobby, skidded across the highly-polished tiled floor and stopped right behind several large ornamental plant pots. Consisting of half a dozen yucca plants, a couple of large palm trees and a selection of large indoor cactus plants, they thankfully hid the case and its passengers from the staff sat behind the reception desk, currently checking people into their rooms.

Getting off the case, Fluke stepped backwards, right into a very prickly cactus tree. 'Ouch!' he yelped, 'that hurt!'

'Turn around Fluke, and let's have a look,' laughed Tash, and watched as Fluke spun himself around for Tash to locate the prickly thorn. She plucked the offending cactus spike out, and, still chuckling, she said, 'you'll have to be more careful next time, and not walk backwards.'

'Come on,' said Elfonzo, eager to get going, 'let's head up to room 301 and rescue Santa's time-freezing machine before it's too late.'

'You're right, Elfonzo,' said Tash. 'C'mon Fluke, grab our case and let's head over there...' Tash moved one of the palm tree leaves aside, and indicated with her paw, '...to those lifts. It's much quicker than walking up three flights of stairs.'

They waited for the right opportunity, when they thought nobody was watching, and stepped out from behind the pot plants and into the main hotel lobby. They tried to blend in with the hotel guests and were stood patiently in line waiting for one of the lifts to arrive when they heard a voice behind them.

'Excuse me...' the official sounding voice was getting louder as the person got closer. Tash turned round to see who was speaking. 'Yoo-Hoo! Hello there...' the official looking man was trying to get someone's attention and continued, 'yes, you three, yes you...' the man indicated with his pointing finger towards Tash, '...you three stood by the lifts in fancy dress Elf costumes, have you checked in yet?'

'Us?' said Tash, trying to figure out how they were going to explain why they were stood in line for the lifts, dressed as Elves.

'Please follow me back to the reception desk, we'll have you checked in in no time at all,' said the man cheerfully, guiding Fluke, Tash and Elfonzo back to his desk.

Tash leant on the desk, trying to act cool and play the part of a hotel guest. Fluke was stood next to her and spied the man's name badge.

'Hi Gus,' said Fluke, taking over the conversation. He'd seen a guest book on the desk, upside down, and thankfully opened up at the page for room 301. He'd quickly read some typed notes alongside Bah Humbug's name, hoping his *reading upside down* ability was good enough to convince the receptionist, he continued, 'We're here to see a Mr. Bah Humbug in room 301. We're representatives from SantaToyz Ltd, you may have heard of us?' Fluke said confidently, hoping the bluff would fool the alert receptionists.

Gus was flustered. Nobody, and especially someone from a large and important company like SantaToyz, had ever called him by his first name before. 'Oh, so that explains the costumes then, ' he indicated the Elf outfits they were wearing, 'very realistic,' he nodded his approval, 'and that's why Mr Bah Humbug was also wearing an Elf costume as well, we did wonder, didn't we Meredith,' he said, turning to his pretty colleague sat next to him.

Meredith checked the notes that had been typed alongside room 301. 'We can see that Mr Bah Humbug has ordered some food on room service,' she smiled at Fluke, 'quite a bit of food actually,' as she studied her notes again. 'We knew he was expecting guests, and looking at the amount he's ordered there should more than enough for you all,' she said happily, 'I'll just tick the box to say you've arrived.' Meredith looked towards the lifts and then said, 'if you hurry along you can share the same lift as the food trolley…' she indicated with a swish of her hand, 'as that's Mr Bah Humbug's food ready to be delivered now,' she pointed towards two waiters pushing an overflowing food trolley, waiting patiently by the lift doors.

'Thank you, Meredith,' said Tash, 'we'll pop up now then, if that's OK? No need to let Mr Bah Humbug know we're here, he is expecting us after all,' said Tash. The three of them hurried over to the lifts and squeezed in, alongside the trolley.

As the lift reached the third floor, the doors opened and they all stepped out into the third floor corridor, and onto some very plush carpet. 'We can push the trolley from here if you want?' offered Tash, 'why don't you two go and have a break? We'll ring down to the kitchens when we've finished with your trolley,' she confirmed, and watched as the two delighted waiters rushed off, they weren't going to miss the opportunity of having a crafty break.

'Time for a quick change, Fluke,' said Tash, opening the magic suitcase. She rummaged around for a few seconds and came out with two waiter outfits. They put the new costumes on over their Elf gear, hoping that nobody would step into the corridor and see them. She stashed their suitcase under the trolley.

'Ready?' asked Elfonzo. 'Right, when we get inside the room, locate the time-freezing machine and push the trolley as close as you can to it, just get me within arm's reach,' said Elfonzo as he climbed under the tablecloth which was draped over the trolley and touched the floor either side, completely hiding Elfonzo underneath. He sat on the bottom shelf of the trolley, alongside plates, napkins and the magic suitcase, clutching the bag that he'd brought with him.

'Why?' asked Tash, pushing the trolley along the carpet, 'and what's in the bag by the way, you never did tell us?'

'A fake time-freezing machine,' said Elfonzo's muffled voice from under the tablecloth, 'we had a dummy one made up to see if it would fit in the sleigh. Of course, it doesn't work, but it does look identical, and if I can get close enough I'll swap them around. Bah Humbug will never know the difference,' chuckled Elfonzo.

'Well, he won't know the difference until they try to get it to work,' laughed Fluke, 'I'd love to see the faces of Bah Humbug and the SantaToyz bosses when they realise they've bought a fake!' He started to count down the room numbers, '309; 307; 305; 303 and here we are, room 301,' said Fluke.

Tash stopped the trolley and readied herself. 'OK, are we all ready?' she asked. 'Let's get inside, swap the machine and get out as fast as we can.'

# Room 301...

Bah Humbug was sat on his bed. The TV was on in the background, some music channel by the sounds of it, not as good as Elf FM, the local North Pole radio station, he thought to himself. His mind wandered back to the meeting he was due to have later and he decided to check on his prized possession again. It would be about the tenth time he'd checked it since he'd arrived.

His bag, which had been brought up to his room by the hotel bellboy, was left on the floor by the side of the bed. Reaching down, he opened the drawstring and reached inside, fumbling around until he located his most prized possession. He gingerly took it out of the bag and held it up to the light for a better look. It didn't look much he thought, but all the electronics were inside the box, hidden from view. When this gadget was inserted into Santa's sleigh, that's when all the magic, time-freezing stuff worked.

The knock at the door interrupted his thoughts. 'Room service for Mr Bah Humbug,' the muffled voice from outside in the corridor said.

He released his hold on the time-freezing machine and threw it on the bed, and watched it bounce on the soft mattress. He hurried over to the door, first peeking through the spyhole, again he'd seen this done in the movies, to check who was outside his room. Strange though, he thought, as he couldn't see anybody stood the other side. He shrugged to himself and opened the door anyway.

'About time too,' said Bah Humbug, 'I've been sat here waiting for the food for at least thirty minutes,' he grumbled. 'The food better not be cold. Just wheel the trolley in and unload it on the coffee table,' he said impatiently, eager to get stuck into the trolley full of food. 'Aren't you two a bit short to be waiters?' asked Bah Humbug, but he was instantly distracted when he lifted the silver lids from some of the serving dishes and started helping himself to some chips.

'OK sir,' said Tash, who promptly wheeled the trolley over to the bed instead of the coffee table. 'The music channel sounds good sir,' she said trying to distract Bah Humbug's attention whilst Elfonzo reached out from under the trolley to swap the machines over.

'Not there!' said Bah Humbug angrily. 'Does that bed really look like a coffee table? I told you to wheel it over there,' he huffed and pointed to the small table. He then stomped impatiently around the room, watching as Tash wheeled the trolley over and helped Fluke transfer the food onto the small table.

'OK Mr Humbug, if you could phone down to reception when you've finished, and someone will be back to collect the dirty dishes,' said Fluke.

'Bah Humbug, *NOT* Humbug,' he tutted, 'you just can't get the staff these days. Well, I hope you two don't come back and clear the dishes, and that they send somebody with more manners,' said Bah Humbug, munching a mouthful of chips.

'Don't you worry sir, I have a feeling you won't see us again, but I think we might be seeing you sometime soon,' said Tash as she wheeled the empty trolley out of the door, closely followed by Fluke who slammed the door to room 301 firmly behind him.

What did they mean by *"I think we might be seeing you sometime soon"* Bah Humbug thought to himself? He soon forgot all about it and began tucking into his dinner, but only after carefully placing his prized possession back into his bag on the floor.

Fluke and Tash lifted the corner of the large tablecloth and peered under the trolley to see a grinning Elfonzo.

'Well?' asked Fluke.

'Well what?' smiled Elfonzo.

'Did you manage to swap the machines over?' Both Fluke and Tash said at the same time.

'Of course I did!' said Elfonzo and leapt onto the carpet, dragging Fluke and Tash's magic suitcase with him.

'Job done!' grinned Fluke. 'C'mon then, we'd better get out of here, before old Bah Humbug discovers we've switched machines, and head back to the Christmas village. Santa will be happy, very happy indeed, especially as Christmas now doesn't need to be cancelled!'

## 22nd December

# Christmas is saved...

Fluke, Tash and Elfonzo returned back to Santa's Christmas village as heroes. A warm welcoming committee had been waiting patiently in the packed dormitory.

'We did it Santa...' said an excited Fluke, breathlessly, 'we rescued the time-freezing machine. Elfonzo swapped it for a fake one that he'd made in toy making class, Bah Humbug will never be able to spot the difference, it looked exactly the same and even fooled us it was that good.'

'You two had the hard bit,' said Elfonzo cheerily, 'you had to keep Bah Humbug talking, while all I had to do was hide under the trolley and swap the machines around.'

'You all played your part,' said Santa happily, 'the three of you have been amazing, Christmas is saved!' continued Santa. 'OK everybody,' he said, clapping his hands happily, and turning to the room full of Elves, 'back to work! We've got a lot to do in the next two days,' and watched with pride as the Elves filed out of the dormitory chatting excitedly as they headed off to various parts of the village to finish last minute jobs.

'What can we do to help, Santa?' asked Tash, very happy they'd managed to save Christmas.

'Where do I start, Tash?' exclaimed Santa. 'Well, first I have to do a quick check on the *naughty and nice* list, then we have to get the presents over to the sleigh; the reindeer need grooming and last minute health checks; I need a weather forecast from the Elf HQ – Traffic and Weather Centre, that's very important; the sleigh needs to be checked over and stocked full of food for myself *and* the reindeer, they need their high energy food to keep flying all night long, it's too long a night to go without eating,' continued Santa, 'although Mrs Claus does prepares me a lovely packed lunch,' he chuckled.

'Don't you eat mince pies, cookies and milk at every house?' asked Fluke, suddenly interested at the mention of snacking.

Santa gave a deep belly laugh, 'Ho, ho, ho. Of course I do Fluke, all those children leave me food at night, its very kind of them.'

'And carrots for the reindeer?' asked Tash

'Oh yes,' said Santa, 'eating carrots is good for you and helps with your eyesight. Very useful when flying the sleigh at night in the dark, let me tell you.'

The list of essential things that needed doing before Christmas Eve was staggering. It made Fluke and Tash realise just how much work was involved here in Santa's workshop village.

# 23rd December

# Packing the sleigh...

It was agreed that Fluke and Tash would pop over to the workshop and help the Elves check the presents, sort them into the correct order and get them over to the sleigh. Santa would check on the reindeer.

Tash opened the huge doors to the workshop. Fluke followed, and they both witnessed a scene so hectic and noisy they could barely hear themselves talk over the din.

They spotted Elfonzo, Winterfluff, Fizzylights, Candysocks, Fairylights, Ivycrystals and Winterbaubles all stood over the far end. They were taking presents off a large table, checking the naughty and nice list, double checking the gift tag name on the present, and when satisfied they placed the presents onto a large conveyor belt.

Striding over, Tash offered them a helping hand.

'Thanks for coming over to help,' said Elfonzo cheerily. 'Grab this list,' he said, and handed Tash a large sheet of paper, full of names. 'You need to check that each of the presents on the table behind you has the right name on it,' he indicated behind him with his thumb at the overflowing table of gift wrapped presents. 'And then we've got to load the presents on the conveyor belt in the right order. It's very important or else Santa might deliver the wrong present to the wrong child!' Elfonzo said and turned back to the fast moving conveyor belt.

Fluke peered over Tash's shoulder, and took a look at the long list of names. 'Tom, James, Max, Wendy, Misty, Sophie...' the list went on and on. Fluke reached over to the table, checked the first present was labelled to Tom, and placed it on the conveyor belt. Tash reached behind her and grabbed the present for James and copied Fluke. They watched in awe as the presents were whisked away on the conveyor belt and disappeared through a flap at the end of the line.

Fluke and Tash were working at full steam. An endless line of presents were being placed on the conveyor belt. Fluke reached behind him and grabbed the latest present, carefully gift wrapped and noted the gift tag. 'Hey Tash, look! I've got a present here for "Meredith", do you reckon it's the helpful lady at the hotel's reception desk?' he chuckled and threw the present onto the conveyor belt.

Sadly for Fluke, this time his aim wasn't that good. The red, silver and blue gift wrapped parcel, decked out with Christmas trees and holly, had partly slipped off the edge of the belt and got stuck, totally wedged and stopped moving. It was also stopping all the other presents from further up the line passing by and was beginning to cause an almighty back log.

Now, climbing onto a moving conveyor belt might seem fun, but is in fact very, very dangerous and something you should never do. Ever. There were warning signs everywhere, plastered all over the walls. Holly Wreath, the Elf and Safety Officer, would go mad if she knew what was about to happen. Fluke read the signs "Do not touch the conveyor belt"; "Do not climb on the conveyor belt" and began to panic. Presents were piling up and causing a blockage.

Fluke checked that nobody was watching, and clambered up onto the conveyor belt. *What could go wrong? I'll only be a few seconds,* he thought to himself, as he hopped up and wiggled the present. It loosened itself and the conveyor belt, with a massive jolt, started moving again. The sudden movement caused Fluke to lose his balance. He stumbled and fell backwards, laid on his back staring up at the moving ceiling.

Tash, unaware of the problems, had thrown a huge present onto the belt. As she looked up, she witnessed the present land on Fluke who was trying to get up. He was unable to move and was being whisked down the line. More and more presents were being piled up on top of him.

'Fluke! Quick, get off the belt,' shouted Tash.

It was no good. Fluke was unable to move.

Turning to Elfonzo, Tash shouted above the din, 'You've got to help, look...' she pointed with her paw, 'Fluke's right down the other end of the room on the conveyor belt.'

Elfonzo saw what was happening, but was a split second too late. He was about to press the Emergency Stop button when they all saw Fluke, and the presents, disappear through the flap at the end of the line. He was gone. Vanished from sight.

A collective gasp spread around the room. A clearly worried Tash broke the silence. 'Err, so now what happens to Fluke?' she asked. 'Where does the conveyor belt lead to?'

Elfonzo shook his head. 'I'm afraid it leads directly to Santa's sleigh, and I would say right now Tash, that Fluke has disappeared inside Santa's magic, bottomless, red sack, with thousands of presents piling on top of him.'

'Oh crikey!' exclaimed Tash. 'Fluke's going to get gift wrapped and be given away as a present. That'll certainly be a surprise for someone! They'll have asked for a push bike and instead they'll get a daft, spotty Dalmatian! C'mon, we've got to try and rescue him,' said Tash, and hurried from the room.

# Poorly reindeer...

Santa, Winter Sleigh and Ivy Sleigh stood around, shaking their heads, looking worried. They glanced over to Smelf, the doctor from the National Elf Service, who was checking and tending to the sick reindeer. He had his medical bag open on the stable floor. Rummaging around inside, he took out a thermometer, stuck it in Dancer's mouth and waited a few seconds before he checked the results.

'What's the matter with them?' asked a concerned Santa, stroking the fur of Randolph and Dancer, who had both tried to stand on wobbly legs when Santa arrived. It was obvious that both reindeer were poorly.

'As you know Santa,' said Smelf, 'Randolph's been ill for a few days now, and yesterday Dancer started showing signs of sickness as well. They have a temperature...' he said checking the thermometer one more time, 'and the flu virus is spreading.'

'Flu? So my reindeer have flu?' queried Santa, clearly shocked.

'I'm afraid so, but thankfully it's not too serious. They'll be as right as rain in a few days' time, all they need is plenty of rest, to be kept warm and be well fed.'

'We don't have a few days to spare, Smelf. In case you hadn't realised Christmas Eve is tomorrow,' sighed Santa.

'They're not well enough to fly, Santa. They won't make it, and certainly not in this weather,' Smelf indicated outside the barn where a wintry blizzard was in full force.

'Are any of the young reindeer trainee recruits fit and ready as replacements?' asked Santa, turning hopefully to Winter Sleigh.

Winter Sleigh looked over to Ivy Sleigh, and they both shook their heads. 'They're still a few months away from being ready, sorry Santa,' said Winter Sleigh.

'Well, unless we can come up with a plan, and quickly, everybody's hard work through the year will be in vain. We can't pull the sleigh with two reindeer missing,' said Santa, deep in thought.

'Err Santa...' said Ivy Sleigh, 'I might just have a plan,' he said grinning from ear to ear.

'Plan? What plan?' asked Santa hopefully.

'Well, I've seen them fly and Elfonzo hasn't stopped going on about them all day. If we manage to strap them into a harness....' He whispered to himself, carefully thinking things through, 'it might just work...' said Ivy Sleigh, his voice trailing off.

'Who?' said Santa, 'Who can we harness to help pull the sleigh...?'

# Inside Santa's magic sack...

It all happened so quickly that Fluke didn't have time to think, let alone try to save himself. One second he was underneath a pile of Christmas presents on the conveyor belt, and the next he was dropping rapidly through the air. He'd reached the end of the moving conveyor, when he, along with all the presents, dropped off the end and began tumbling downwards, heading for a large red sack, its top wide open, gratefully receiving thousands upon thousands of presents.

Once Fluke's free fall stopped, he found himself sat upon gift wrapped presents of all shapes and sizes. Red, silver, blue and green wrapping paper surrounded him. Some had Santa and his reindeer on the paper, some had Christmas trees, and there was an assortment of snowflakes, baubles and tinsel.

He looked up at the opening way above him, and watched as several more presents tumbled off the conveyor, dropped into the sack and nestled alongside him, narrowly missing bopping him on the head. Thankfully it stopped raining presents and Fluke began wondering how he could climb out.

'Why don't I ever follow instructions,' he muttered to himself, clambering over several presents, trying desperately not to squash any. The thought that any children would get damaged gifts this Christmas because Fluke had been careless, and sat or trod on them, made him shudder. 'The sign clearly said "Do not touch the conveyor belt" and "Do not climb on the conveyor belt", but noooo, I always think I know best,' said Fluke, telling himself off.

Fluke eventually reached the side of the sack, reached out with his paws and felt soft cloth. Gazing around, he was amazed. The size of the sack was way bigger on the inside than it was on the outside. He gave up trying to work it out, as Santa's sack was obviously magic. *Well, it makes sense when you think about it, it has to be huge to hold thousands of presents,* thought Fluke.

The sides of the sack were red, smooth and very, very soft to the touch. There was no way he could climb the sides. He had an idea and started to build a tower of presents. Starting with the biggest one he could find, he read the gift tag and noted it was to "Sophie". 'Sorry Sophie,' he muttered, 'hope I don't squash or damage your present.' Finding a slightly smaller one, he placed this on top. This carried on for a few minutes, his tower of presents was getting taller as more and more were added.

Fluke started climbing up the tower of wrapped presents with more parcels under each arm, placing one on top of the other. He eventually reached the halfway point when the tower began to rock back and forth. With nothing to hang on to he couldn't stop the swaying and his impressive tower of presents came tumbling down, to form a not so impressive mound of presents scattered everywhere back at the bottom of Santa's sack.

'Fluke? Are you in there?' said a familiar voice from way above.

'Tash? Is that you? Err, I think I need some help to get me out of here. I'm stuck and can't climb the sides,' wailed Fluke, looking upwards to the opening. He caught sight of a head looking over the edge and realised with relief that it was indeed Tash peering down.

# Rope climbing...

'Don't move Fluke, I'll be back in a minute.' Tash's face disappeared from view. Fluke waited, and waited a bit more, until eventually Fluke heard sounds of giggling coming from above. Looking towards the light at the top of the sack, Fluke saw several faces peering down. He recognised Elfonzo, Winterfluff and several other Elves peeking over the edge, pointing and laughing.

Tash came back into the room carrying a large bundle of knotted rope. 'Help me unroll this will you, Elfonzo?' asked Tash, 'I hope it's long enough,' she said and dropped one end inside Santa's magic red sack. Carefully feeding the rope through her paws until there was only a little bit left, Tash and six Elves held their end, just like a tug of war team. 'Fluke, can you see the rope?' asked Tash.

'Yes!' replied Fluke. He had been sat patiently on a pile of presents, watching as the knotted rope dropped and dangled right in front of his face.

'Good. Well grab hold of the end and start climbing. If you can't, we'll have to pull you out,' she instructed and waited.

'OK, I'm climbing up now,' came Fluke's muffled reply.

They took the strain and held on firmly.

Fluke grabbed hold and began the tricky climb to safety. Paw over paw, he began his ascent. Looking up he saw with relief the top was getting closer until eventually he was helped back over the edge by strong Elf hands, and flopped back onto the workshop floor.

Looking all around, the person he saw first was a worried looking Santa.

'Are you OK, Fluke?' asked Santa, helping Fluke get to his paws and dusting him down.

'Yep, I'm fine,' confirmed Fluke. 'I'm really, really sorry about that. I was only trying to help you know, the present got stuck and I was trying to wiggle it free and then....'

'Whoa! You're safe, that's all I'm worried about,' interrupted Santa smiling.

'There is one small thing though, Santa,' said Fluke sheepishly.

'What's that, Fluke?' said Santa

'Well, when you deliver a present to "Sophie", it might be a tiny bit squashed as I sat on it, so, if you see her, can you apologise from me?'

Santa laughed, 'I'm sure its fine, Fluke. Now I have a favour to ask you two...' he said pointing to both Fluke and Tash, 'I, well *we,* all of us in fact, need your help again.'

'OK,' said Tash, looking firstly to Santa and then over to Fluke, 'how can we help?'

'We need you and your magic suitcase to lead the sleigh team tomorrow night.'

# 24th December...

The singing Elf clock on the wall chimed twelve times to introduce midnight, a new day, but not just any new day. It was Christmas Eve.

Tash looked around the packed room, the last few hours had whizzed by. Once Fluke had been rescued from Santa's magic sack, the Elves quickly got back to work. The conveyor belt started working again and finished the important job of filling the sack full to the brim with presents for children all around the world.

The reindeer team, led in by Winter Sleigh and Ivy Sleigh, proudly took their places in front of the gleaming new, highly-polished sleigh, shaking their impressive antlers in excitement. They were keen to get going after years of training for this, the most important job of the year.

The Sleigh was packed and ready to go, well, very nearly ready to go. There were two empty harnesses at the front where the two poorly reindeer, Randolph and Dancer, would normally take their places.

Fluke had disappeared back to the dormitory, returning a few minutes later carrying their magic case.

Winter Sleigh helped fit the magic case into the harness and watched as Tash leapt up onto the front, closely followed by Fluke who was sat in his usual spot right behind, peeking over her shoulder. They were both wearing goggles, having first made sure that they were de-iced and fitted correctly. They couldn't afford any mistakes, today of all days. A lot rested on their shoulders, and the importance of the occasion suddenly dawned on Fluke, who was a tiny bit nervous.

Tapping Tash on the shoulder, he asked 'Are you ready, Tash?'

'As ready as we can be, Fluke,' said Tash. 'This is going to be one very, very exciting trip. I mean, who would have thought we'd be leading the sleigh, helping Santa deliver all these presents!'

Elfonzo was watching from the sidelines. Santa looked over from his seat in the sleigh and chuckled. 'Well, are you coming then?' and watched as a delighted Elfonzo, beaming from ear to ear, leapt up onto the case and sat snuggly behind Fluke.

# Leading the sleigh...

Fluke, Tash and the reindeer carefully led the sleigh out of the large double doors at the far end of the workshop. Santa was sat at the controls, pressing buttons and flicking switches. He'd received the weather report from the Elf HQ – Traffic and Weather Centre. High winds and plenty of snow were forecast for the North Pole. The weather was improving over parts of North America and Europe, Africa was going to be hot and so was Australia.

The sleigh was followed outside by hundreds of cheering, happy Elves, who stood watching, whistling and applauding. This was a magical sight, 364 days of hard work to reach this day, Christmas Eve.

The sleigh stopped. Tash stared into the darkness, but couldn't see very far ahead, even with her fantastic eyesight. A few seconds later however, they were all dazzled by powerful lights. Somebody had flicked a switch, turning total darkness temporarily into daylight. Two long lines of bright lights stretched away and disappeared off into the distance. The sleigh was parked at the top of a long runway, the runway lights guiding the way forward. The reindeer and Elves were waiting patiently for Santa to start the countdown.

At the last moment, Mrs Claus ran towards the sleigh and handed Santa his packed lunch. 'Just in case nobody leaves you any mince pies or cookies...' she said to Santa, 'it'll be a long night dearest, we can't have you going hungry now, can we?'

Santa looked bashful as he stored the sandwiches in the sleigh glovebox. 'Thank you dear,' he said, 'OK, are we ready to start the countdown?' he asked.

Fluke gave the thumbs up sign. Tash, Elfonzo and the reindeer all nodded. Time to go.

A hush filled the cold night air when suddenly a screeching noise came out of speakers mounted on the outside wall of the workshop.

'Err, apologies about that,' said Elfis, Elf FM's DJ, his voice booming over the speaker system. 'We had a slight technical issue with the countdown clock, but we're ready to go now. So please, everybody, join in the traditional countdown,' and his voice started to shout out the numbers. Every Elf joined Elfis in the countdown, their voices mingled with the public address speakers as they began chanting together, the excitement growing – "*Ten, nine, eight, seven, six, five, four, three, two, one,"* and when the final number was called the Elves cheered loudly. The reindeer, led by Fluke, Tash and Elfonzo, shot down the runway, building up speed. The Elves watched in awe as the sleigh took to the air. Santa did a full circle and flew directly overhead, waving to the watching Elves stood below.

# First stop, New Zealand...

Santa turned on the time-freezing machine, and then the sat nav. He fiddled with some buttons, flicked switches and turned dials. 'How're things up front?' he hollered above the wind.

Fluke's ears were flapping wildly in the strong winds, but he managed to turn around and shout back, 'cold and windy, but we're OK, aren't we Tash?'

'We're good, Santa,' confirmed Tash. 'The reindeer are fine, aren't you guys?' and she leant over to pat the furry flanks of the closest reindeer. 'Our magic case is fitting in nicely, helping pull the sleigh, and I think we all make a good team! It's such a shame that Randolph and Dancer weren't well enough to fly though, but we're so glad to stand in and help,' continued Tash, her voice just audible above the roaring wind.

'Where to first Santa?' hollered Fluke.

'We have several million stops to make in the South Pacific Islands, onto New Zealand and then Australia,' he confirmed. 'It should also start to get a bit warmer soon,' he shivered, as even Santa felt the cold. He pushed a button on his dashboard, which turned on the heater. He began to wiggle his toes as the heater began to thaw out his cold feet.

The sleigh was in full flight, gradually eating up the miles as they approached their first stop. The time-freezing machine was working perfectly, and as they flew high above in the night sky, Tash looked down at the villages, towns and cities spread below, the street lights twinkling brightly in the dark.

Santa was constantly checking his sat nav, giving Fluke, Tash and the reindeer team some very clear directions, then checking off his naughty and nice list. The present dispensing machine churned out a steady stream of gift wrapped presents, all in the correct order, and all with a name tag. Fluke was now very aware of how important the packing operation had been back in the workshop, where each present had to be placed carefully in the sack, in the correct order.

Santa slowed the sleigh and hovered over each house, disappeared over the edge, only to return milliseconds later and grab the next gift, to disappear again.

Within a short space of time, thanks to the time-freezing machine, the whole of the South Pacific region, which included New Zealand,

Australia and a whole host of smaller islands had successfully had all their presents delivered.

Santa and his team were gradually working their way across the globe, trying to keep ahead of the ticking clock. After Australia, the sleigh headed off to Indonesia, Thailand, China, Russia and all the neighbouring countries. They then continued towards Europe, the reindeer pulling the sleigh must have been exhausted but gave no sign they wanted a break. Years of training gave them the strength needed for a long night's work.

Fluke tapped Tash on the shoulder. 'Do you reckon Santa will let us deliver some presents, Tash? It will certainly help speed things up if we all help, what do you reckon?'

'Don't see why not Fluke, makes sense to me,' she replied above the howling wind. 'Santa?' she shouted over Fluke and Elfonzo's shoulders, 'any chance we can help deliver some presents?'

'Of course you can, I thought you'd never ask!' chuckled Santa.

# Special delivery...

S anta slowed down the sleigh, and parked up on a quiet snow-filled street. He couldn't see any double yellow lines, although the thick snow may have hidden them and, more importantly, he didn't spy any traffic wardens lurking around the corner either. It still confused Santa as to how the time-freezing machine hadn't affected the traffic warden like other people and slow him down enough to stop him from issuing a parking ticket. Santa was still getting stick from Mrs Claus about that night – fancy that, Santa getting a fine!

All was silent, the air very cold but still. Fluke hopped down from the case, stretched his stiff legs and was followed by Tash and Elfonzo.

'I know we're in England Santa, but whereabouts are we exactly?' asked Tash, unable to get her bearings.

'Devon, Tash, we're near the seaside, but we don't have time for a trip to the beach or a paddle I'm afraid,' chuckled Santa. He checked his list and reached inside his sack for the next presents on the list and handed one to Fluke, one to Tash and one to Elfonzo.

'I've got Tom's,' said Fluke, checking the gift tag.

'Well, mine's for James,' confirmed Tash, carefully checking her bulky gift wrapped item.

'And I've got one for Bobby,' said Elfonzo, studying his present which was bone shaped and squeaked when he squeezed the present. 'Do you think Bobby is the family dog by any chance?' laughed Elfonzo.

'Must be why Santa didn't give that one to Fluke to deliver!' chuckled Tash. 'Poor old Bobby would've had a broken, plastic bone without a squeak for Christmas, if Fluke had gotten to it first. He's managed to wreck every squeaky toy he's ever been given!' said Tash, continuing to laugh and make fun of Fluke.

'Ha-ha,' said Fluke, 'you two are *soooo* not funny, I hope Santa's got you a new joke book for Christmas. Come on then, we better get inside and deliver the presents.'

'Not so fast,' said Santa, walking over to the waiting trio. 'I've got to sprinkle you with magic dust or else you might not get inside the house,' he said. Reaching into his deep pocket he withdrew a handful of gold coloured dust which he sprinkled over the heads of Fluke, Tash and Elfonzo.

'Now what?' asked Tash. 'How do we get in?'

'Duh! Down the chimney, Tash,' said Fluke, brushing off the excess dust from his Elf costume, 'everybody knows Santa goes down the chimney!'

'I know that, but not all houses have a chimney, Fluke,' said Tash, shaking her head.

'Ah, and that's where the magic dust comes in handy,' interrupted Santa, 'it shrinks you down, if you need to, so you can slip in under the door, or through any duct or vent. Every house has a small access point somewhere,' he continued. 'But you're in luck,' he pointed up to the roof, 'they have a chimney here, so off you go. I'll feed the reindeer whilst you're inside. Remember, leave the presents under the Christmas tree and get out quickly,' and he watched as Fluke, Tash and Elfonzo climbed up onto the roof and hesitated around the chimney stack.

# Mince pies and cookies...

Fluke, Tash and Elfonzo were stood around the chimney stack, but none of them wanted to be the first to climb down into the dark interior.

'You first,' said Fluke, shoving Tash in the back, propelling her closer to the lip of the chimney and causing her to slip on the roof tiles.

'Oh thanks!' said Tash, steadying herself, before peering down into the darkness below. She climbed up and sat on the chimney pot, her paws dangling over the edge. 'Pass me the present then,' she asked, and waited patiently for Elfonzo to hand her James's present. Tash hesitated for a second, and then started to climb down inside, one paw clutched the present, and the other held onto the side wall.

'I hope the fire isn't going and that they've swept the chimney,' chuckled Fluke. 'Oh, and mind the dog, Bobby might just be waiting for you!' Thankfully Fluke couldn't hear Tash's muffled reply coming from halfway down the chimney.

Next up was Elfonzo. Being the smallest he found it easy. Jumping up onto the edge, he eased himself into the chimney pot and disappeared from sight, leaving Fluke standing on the roof. Looking down to Santa feeding the reindeer, he noticed Santa look up. Fluke gave him the thumbs up sign and edged slowly to the chimney pot.

'Now or never,' he mumbled to himself and climbed over the edge. To say it was dark inside was the biggest understatement ever. It was pitch black. Fluke found the edge of the chimney wall and began to climb down, slowly, very, very slowly. He carefully edged himself down towards the fireplace below, the descent was going well until the chimney flue began to narrow. 'Tash,' he whispered urgently. Nothing. No response. 'Tash,' he whispered a bit louder, 'I need a hand. I'm stuck!'

He heard Elfonzo sniggering below, and sounds of eating.

'Hang on in there Fluke, let us finish these mince pies and cookies first,' chuckled Tash between mouthfuls of food. 'These home-baked mince pies are the best I've ever eaten, you should try one.'

'Yeah, yeah, stop munching and get me down. I can't stay here all night,' whined Fluke, as he struggled to free himself.

'Drop the present Fluke, I'll catch it and then we'll help you get down,' laughed Elfonzo. Fluke did as instructed and thankfully heard Elfonzo catch Tom's present.

Fluke breathed in as far as he could and felt himself slip a little bit. He then felt a pair of hands on one leg and a pair of paws on the other.

'On the count of three we'll pull you down,' said Tash. 'Ready?' she asked, and started the countdown. *'One, two, three!'*

Fluke felt his body slip through the narrow opening and he fell the last few feet, landing in the fireplace, which thankfully wasn't lit. He sat there staring around the room. He then heard a slight rumbling from above, but before he could move, a plume of coal dust came tumbling down the chimney and covered him from head to paw in black soot.

'Didn't know you wanted to become a chimney sweep, Fluke,' laughed Tash. She laughed even louder when Fluke stepped out of the fireplace and headed over to the Christmas tree. The fairy lights had been left on, a soft glow came from the twinkling lights, and as Fluke stepped over to deliver his present Tash caught sight of him. 'Don't leave sooty paw prints on the carpet, Fluke!'

The presents were successfully delivered, and Fluke looked desperately around the room. 'Where's the mince pies then?' he asked.

''Err, we've eaten them,' said Tash.

'What, all of them?' replied a horrified Fluke.

'Pretty much all of them,' said Elfonzo and passed Fluke the empty plate.

'You've not even saved me one cookie or mince pie?' complained Fluke.

'We've saved you a carrot though, Fluke,' chuckled Tash. 'Think about it, you nearly got stuck coming down the chimney and we've got to climb back up again in a minute, so the less you eat the easier it will be to get out again.'

'How did you manage to get stuck, Fluke?' asked Elfonzo, 'Santa covered us all in magic dust remember?'

Fluke looked bashful, 'I brushed it off before we climbed down!'

'Are you three coming back up, or are you staying here for Christmas?' said a voice floating down the chimney.

'C'mon! Santa's up on the roof. We better get moving,' said Elfonzo, and watched as Tash shinnied up the chimney. Elfonzo was next. Last, as always, was Fluke, who struggled up the chimney. He was given a helping hand by Santa, Tash and Elfonzo. All three tugged and pulled, then watched as Fluke popped out of the chimney like a cork from a champagne bottle.

They leapt aboard their case and waited for Santa to climb into his sleigh. He set the sat nav. 'OK,' he hollered, 'we're off,' and the sleigh, pulled by the magic case and the reindeer, took to the air and gracefully headed off to the next houses on the list.

# A job well done...

Santa stood leaning against his sleigh, ruffling the furry heads of his team of reindeer. Turning to his companions he said, 'well, another successful year! Everybody on the list has had their presents delivered in record time.'

'I think we can say it's a job well done,' said Fluke happily.

'That magic case of yours…' Santa said looking at Fluke and Tash, 'is amazing and certainly helped. Can I borrow it next year?' he laughed.

'Where too now then, Santa?' asked Tash.

'Home; back to our Christmas village for a celebration. It's tradition you know,' confirmed Santa, 'whilst we've been out delivering, Mrs Claus, Nigelfa and the rest of the Elves have been setting up for tonight's party.'

'What are we waiting for?' said Fluke gleefully, 'we love a good party, don't we Tash?' He quickly joined Tash and Elfonzo on the case, then watched as Santa leapt into his sleigh.

'No need for the sat nav now,' chuckled Santa, 'these reindeer know the route back home,' and with a tug on the reins, the reindeer pulled the sleigh along the ground, building up speed before they all lifted into the air. Destination: The North Pole, Christmas village.

# A night to remember...

As the sleigh came into land on the runway they were greeted by hundreds of cheering, happy Elves and given a hero's welcome. The reindeer led the sleigh back into the workshop, the double doors at the far end were closed, keeping the cold out.

Mrs Claus emerged from the crowd and hugged Santa. 'You look tired dearest,' she said, 'but the party should perk you up!' and she led everybody through to the canteen.

Nigelfa and Mrs Claus had prepared a feast. Tables were groaning under the weight of party food, and Elfis had picked some fine sounding music to listen to as Elf FM radio played through the speakers.

The party was in full swing. Fluke, Tash and Elfonzo mingled and were speaking to Winterfluff and Candysocks, reliving the night of adventure and excitement, when the music stopped playing and an announcement from Elfis came over the radio.

'*Santa to the telephone please, Santa to the telephone, I have an urgent message for you,*' said

Elfis's voice through the speakers. Santa put his plate of food back on the table and went over to the telephone fixed to the wall. Lifting the receiver he dialled the number which fed him through to the Elf FM studio.

'What's that about?' asked Tash, as the music started playing again.

Elfonzo shrugged his shoulders, 'not sure Tash, but Santa's nodding his head to whatever Elfis is telling him.' They watched as Santa replaced the telephone handset and walked back over.

Newsflash…

Santa cleared his throat and prepared to make a short announcement. 'If I could have your attention for a minute please…' he said loudly and waited patiently for the hubbub of noise to quieten down. 'We need to put the TV on for a short while, we have some interesting news to share.'

All heads turned to the large TV fixed on the wall and waited in silence for the television screen to turn on. Disappointed groans filled the room as the TV refused to work.

'No signal,' said Tash, looking at the little message on the dark screen.

Santa fiddled with the batteries in the remote control, turned the TV off and then back on again. This time the screen swam into life, and the happy, cheering Elves quietened again as the screen showed a live news broadcast.

A reporter was stood in a familiar looking reception area and speaking into a microphone. 'Here we are, live from the foyer at the Ritz Hotel, London,' the reporter said.

'Look, Fluke,' said Tash pointing to the screen, 'that's the hotel we went to, and there's Meredith stood behind the reception desk.'

'An arrest has been made by the local Police,' continued the reporter, 'a man pretending to be an Elf from Santa's workshop claimed to have Santa's time-freezing machine and attempted to sell it to a company called SantaToyz Ltd. The machine proved to be a fake, and SantaToyz Ltd called the police...'

Gasps of shock and horror came from the watching Elves as they witnessed Bah Humbug being led away in a set of handcuffs, escorted out of the reception and into a waiting Police van.

Flash light bulbs filled the night sky; a bunch of newspaper photographers jostled with each other, each one hoping for the perfect picture which would make the front of tomorrow's newspapers. The last image on the TV screen was of Bah Humbug sat in the Police van, handcuffed to a burly looking Policeman. Santa turned the TV off, and said sadly 'Well, that just goes to prove that crime doesn't pay.'

The music started up again, and the party continued. Fluke was looking at the large Elf clock on the wall, and nudged Tash. 'Look Tash, it's nearly midnight, Christmas Day is only a few seconds away.'

Santa started the official countdown. 'Ten; Nine; Eight; Seven,' everybody had now joined in with the counting, '*Six, Five, Four, Three, Two, One. Happy Christmas!*' And they all cheered, patting each other on the backs and clinking glasses together in celebration.

Santa had arranged for the official photographer, Selfie, to line everybody up for the annual Christmas photograph. When he was happy that everybody was in the shot, he set the timer and joined Fluke and Tash kneeling at the front.

'Say *CHEEZE*,' laughed Fluke. The flash went off capturing the photo, and Selfie rushed off to get the picture developed.

## 25th December

# Christmas Day...

Tash was the first to wake. She gazed around the dormitory and noted that Fluke, along with all the Elves, was still busy snoring. It had been a late night, the party went on till the early hours of the morning. One by one the Elves woke and the normal hubbub of noise filled the room.

Tash shook Fluke and gently woke him. 'C'mon sleepyhead, time to get up.'

'Oh, I was having a wonderful dream about our night out with Santa,' said Fluke dreamily, 'whizzing around the world on our case, being part of the reindeer team, delivering presents, it was a fantastic experience,' he sighed.

'Yeah, well now it's time to go home,' said Tash.

'Have we got time for one of Nigelfa's Christmas dinners, Tash?' asked Fluke hopefully.

'There's always time for another of Nigelfa's special dinners, Fluke,' said Tash, and she leapt out of bed to join the Elves leaving the dormitory. 'Last one in the canteen is a looser,' she said and scampered after Elfonzo, leaving Fluke struggling to keep up.

The canteen, as always, was full. The Elves worked 364 days a year, so today, Christmas Day, was their holiday, and they were enjoying their day off.

A set of tables had been set in the middle of the room, and every Elf from the Christmas village was present, sat around the edge and tucking into a hearty Christmas dinner.

# Home time...

After dinner, Fluke went to grab their magic case and found Tash, who had wandered over to see Santa to say their farewells.

'Time for us to go,' she said sadly. 'It's been amazing and we've had a great adventure, haven't we, Fluke?'

'One of the best!' agreed Fluke.

'We're so glad you came, aren't we dearest,' said Santa turning to Mrs Claus, 'and from all of us here...' he indicated around the room to the watching Elves, '...we want to thank you both for helping to save Christmas. Oh, and by the way, if you want to lend us your magic suitcase for next year that would be great,' he chuckled.

Everybody filed out of the canteen and headed to the workshop. The double doors at the end were opened, a draughty wind whistled through, filling the room with snow. Fluke and Tash sat on their magic case at the top of the runway, the controls were set to take them back home to a couple of minutes after they had originally left.

The Elves and Santa cheered heartily as the magic case zoomed down the runway, lifted off the ground, and circled high above. Tash turned the dials on the magic case and they promptly disappeared from sight.

Santa stood gazing up to the empty sky where seconds ago Fluke and Tash had been. 'I'll see you both next year,' he whispered, 'well, as long as you're well-behaved and good that is. I'm sure you'll be on the *nice* list,' and he was led back inside by Mrs Claus.

# 12:24 Christmas morning...

The magic case appeared from out of thin air, skidded across the bedroom carpet and slammed into the wardrobe, causing the doors to fly open and a pile of bed linen and towels to tumble down from the top shelf.

Changing quickly out of the Elf costumes, they stored their case neatly back inside the wardrobe and headed quietly across the landing to the top of the stairs. Creeping down the staircase they peered through the railings and into the living room. The fireplace had some logs burning gently, and the Christmas tree lights twinkled brightly.

'Look Fluke, there's some presents under the tree,' said Tash.

'C'mon, let's have a look then,' and he raced past Tash, down the stairs and skidded to a stop right in front of the tree.

'Santa must have delivered these when our backs were turned, because I don't remember delivering them,' said Tash.

'That present has our names on the gift tag,' said Fluke excitedly, 'we'll open it together Tash, you open one end, and I'll open the other,' he said.

They both ripped the wrapping paper off and sat staring at the box of goodies. 'There's a snow globe of Santa's Christmas village,' said Fluke, who picked it up, gave it a gentle shake and watched in fascination as a mini snowstorm covered the mini village.

'Look closer,' said Tash pointing, 'this is real magic, as every time you shake it a different scene appears. There's one with Mrs Claus, Santa, you and me.' Tash shook it again and a new scene appeared, this time a picture of Fluke and Tash with Elfonzo and the rest of the gang. Fluke took a turn shaking it, and this time it showed Fluke and Tash down at the reindeer training academy, another shake showed them helping Elfski, and then finally a scene with their magic case flying through the air pulling Santa's sleigh with the reindeer team.

'Wow, what a present!' said Tash, 'it's like having our very own story book contained inside this little snow globe, we better hide it and keep it safe.'

Reaching inside the box Fluke pulled out the last item, a large group photograph, the one that Selfie had taken and had printed. Flipping the photo over, they saw Santa had written a personal message, alongside hundreds of signatures from all the Elves.

"To our new friends, Fluke and Tash. We hope you enjoyed your adventure to our Christmas village. Thank you both for helping to save Christmas. We look forward to seeing you next year – Mrs Claus and Santa."